AUDREY'S SEAL (SPECIAL FORCES: OPERATION ALPHA)

JULIA BRIGHT

Dear Readers,

Welcome to the Special Forces: Operation Alpha Fan-Fiction world!

If you are new to this amazing world, in a nutshell the author wrote a story using one or more of my characters in it. Sometimes that character has a major role in the story, and other times they are only mentioned briefly. This is perfectly legal and allowable because they are going through Aces Press to publish the story.

This book is entirely the work of the author who wrote it. While I might have assisted with brainstorming and other ideas about which of my characters to use, I didn't have any part in the process or writing or editing the story.

I'm proud and excited that so many authors loved my characters enough that they wanted to write them into their own story. Thank you for supporting them, and me!

READ ON!
    Xoxo
    Susan Stoker

CHAPTER 1

Tony "Legs" Caruso let out a long groan as he bent low and stretched his hamstrings. Vacation was about relaxing and resting for most people. They came to Hawaii in droves to bake on the beach or by the pool while sipping fruity drinks. That wasn't his style. He'd just finished a six-mile run along the road in front of his hotel in Yosemite, and he was looking forward to a long hike this afternoon.

Everyone on his team had leave they needed to take, but they weren't vacationing together this year. He understood why the guys were going different ways. With the babies in their crew, they wanted to see family. He really was fine with them going their separate ways, though he really liked the guys and surprisingly he liked their women. When Vine had hooked up with Jenna, he'd feared she would ruin their group, but she'd made Vine so happy Legs couldn't resent her.

Legs stood and reached for his foot, pulling it up behind him as he stretched his quads. His gaze swept over the area. The trees were thick, the rocks white and jutting, unlike the black volcanic rocks that made up Hawaii. He dropped his foot and bent low before moving on to stretch the other leg. The first hike they'd taken both Ashley and Jenna's babies on had been interesting. Taking babies anywhere was tricky, but the hike had been good. He really liked those little tykes, even if their presence changed the hikes and their beach days.

He started moving again, wondering if he shouldn't have gone to Tokyo with Quirk. His friend had gone to see a friend stationed there. The alone time here wasn't so bad. It would be nice to have someone to talk to, maybe someone who wanted to rehash the hike or talk about the next one they were going to take. He wanted someone to fish with, someone to chill out beside the campfire with.

No way was he ready for a relationship, though. Sure, the guys seemed happy. Heck, Minx and Sunshine were probably wrapped in each other's arms in some hotel on one of the islands. They got along well, but the last woman Legs had dated had been hell on him. A shiver worked through him, leaving him chilled.

It made him sad that Forest and Becky were getting ready to move to Coronado. They weren't in California yet, so he couldn't stop in for a visit. He would miss working with Astro.

He'd picked this place because he'd wanted something different. Yosemite was nice, and maybe a few weeks away from the group would be good for them all. Soon they'd all be back in Hawaii and life would return to normal.

Legs hadn't driven to the trailhead to start his jog, so he made his way back toward the hotel, taking in the view. This area wasn't what he would call upscale or even good, but he wasn't so special he couldn't bunk for a week in a cheap motel.

Along the path, he found a wrapper for a burger and cup and picked them up, disgusted by how some people thought nothing of junking up nature. He moved to the dumpster at the back of the hotel's property where he was staying. As he drew closer, a noise behind the dumpster made him slow. His stomach muscles tightened as his senses went on alert. Legs went into warrior mode, wishing he had his piece with him.

Legs moved the last few feet silently, then stepped around the back of the cinderblock wall encasing the dumpster, coming face to face with a gun.

"Don't move." The woman's voice shook just like her hands. Her tear-stained face seemed pale and pinched. Almost like she was made of ceramic, but the old type with black cracks showing under the surface. Movement behind the woman grabbed Legs' attention. A dark-haired scamp, maybe four or five, looked out from behind her, fear showing in the kid's eyes.

"Don't want to die," the child whispered, making Legs' gut clench tight.

The woman took one hand off the gun to push the kid back to safety. Legs moved in a flash, taking the gun from the woman, ejecting the clip, and emptying the chamber before the woman had time to scream or move. She sputtered and then cried out in frustration.

"He can't have us back. I won't go!" she yelled as a strangled sob escaped her lips.

Legs raised his hands and his eyebrows. "Whoa, lady, I don't know what you're talking about."

The child looked out from behind the mother, her eyes wide. "Don't kill Mommy."

"I'm not killing anyone," Legs said.

"I saw him—well, I saw someone in the lot early this morning. Stop lying. You're with him."

Quirk looked at the woman's hands. Chipped polish covered most of her short nails, and her dark hair had highlights that looked like they'd grown out. Her shoes looked expensive but rough, like she'd walked too far in them. At one point, he bet she spent a fortune on looking good, but something had changed, driving her to this cheap motel on the edge of civilization.

"Look at me," Legs commanded, using the voice he used when they encountered frightened hostages.

The woman's head snapped up, and her eyes narrowed as she concentrated on him. "I don't know who you are hiding from, but I'm not that person. Come to my room and tell me about everything."

The woman's eyes narrowed, and his lips thinned. He needed to sweeten the deal. He took in her clothes. The mom's clothes were loose, but the young girl's clothes were tight, and her pants were too short.

"I have food. Waffles, cereal, some eggs."

The little girl's eyes grew wide, and she licked her lips. He swore she would have grabbed food from his hands if he had any. The woman didn't look convinced, though.

"I just want to talk."

The fight went out of the woman as she nodded. Legs wanted to shake her. Going to a stranger's hotel room was stupid. He wanted to get some sense into her, but she was all over the place and looked like she might crack at any moment. The look of raw hunger her daughter gave him made him think they had been on the run for a while. This wasn't the life either of them had started with.

Legs led her to his room—the hike could wait—keyed open the door and ushered them inside. He'd opted to rent the suite, which meant he had a kitchenette, a table with three chairs, a couch, and a half wall that separated the bed from the other stuff.

Legs moved his gaze from the woman to the little girl. "My name is Tony, but my friends call me Legs."

"Why?" the girl asked as she clung to her mother's pants leg, her gaze sweeping over him before meeting his gaze again.

Legs lifted an eyebrow, then stuck out one leg and showed the girl his quad. "My muscles, that's why."

The little girl's face scrunched up. "Your leg looks weird."

Legs threw back his head and laughed. The woman jumped at the noise, and he quieted quickly, getting the laughter under control.

"That was rude, Meredith."

Legs shook his head. "It's okay. They do look odd compared to most people. How about some food?"

"We shouldn't," the woman said, her eyes wide as she looked around the room, maybe realizing for the first time she'd gone into a hotel room of a stranger, and she had nothing to defend herself with.

Meredith looked up at him hopefully and nodded. He didn't want to undermine the woman, but he could tell that they both looked hungry, mainly since both of them had been staring a hole through his food on the counter.

"I have bacon—"

Meredith shivered. "I hate bacon."

Legs loved how honest kids were. "I didn't like it until I was older. I do have waffles, and I have some peanut butter. Would you like some eggs and then a waffle with peanut butter?"

Meredith punched the air as she jumped and spun. "Yes!"

The girl's excitement made him smile. He wondered how Oliver and Lila would grow up. Would they be shy or outgoing?

The woman placed her hand on Legs' arm. "You don't have to."

"It's okay." He held her eyes, seeing the worry melt and become tears. She swiped at her eyes before moving to the bathroom and shutting the door.

Legs stepped over to the TV and flipped it on. "Do you like documentaries?" he teased Meredith.

"Yuck. Pappy used to watch those. They're boring."

Another smile curved up his lips. "How about some cartoons? I think this place has the Disney channel."

Meredith nodded furiously and settled on the end of the couch as he flipped channels, searching for something kid appropriate. Meredith settled in when he found the cartoons, looking happy as she watched.

Legs grabbed the bacon from the refrigerator and began frying six strips, then turned his attention to scrambling six eggs. He added two more for good measure, knowing he could eat the extra eggs if Meredith and her mother didn't finish them. They both looked like they were starving and could probably eat all the eggs by themselves.

After he got the eggs into the pan, the bathroom

door opened, and the woman stepped out, her eyes not meeting his as she moved to the kitchen. She looked fragile. Almost like if he talked too loudly, she would shatter. Whatever wrong things were going on in her life, they had pushed her to the edge.

"How can I help?"

"Put two of those waffles from the freezer into the toaster."

She moved to the freezer, and he noticed that her hands still shook. Something bad had gone down in her life, and he had no idea if he could help her.

With breakfast cooked, the mom walked over to turn off the TV, but Legs stopped her. He moved the coffee table so Meredith could watch while she ate.

He flashed the woman a smile, trying to look kinder. He knew he was intense and could easily scare her. "This way, we can sit over here and talk while she eats."

The woman's eyes narrowed, and her lips thinned. She looked ready to say no when her shoulders dropped. Meredith didn't waste any time tucking into the food. She ate like he did after a hard mission, inhaling first, asking questions about what he'd consumed later.

Legs settled at the table with the woman, seeing

that she'd not taken much food. Legs switched their plates and her head whipped up.

"I can't take your food."

He narrowed his eyes, and his lips thinned. "You need more. Besides, I already ate this morning."

"But—"

He waved at her plate. "No buts. Eat more," Legs said, keeping his voice low so Meredith didn't hear.

Her lips thinned out even more as she put eggs on her fork and took a bite. Her eyes closed, and she looked like she might cry again. He'd seen captives like this, starving, upset, so many emotions they couldn't keep it together. He bet Meredith was the only reason this woman was hanging on to whatever thread still held her up.

She opened her eyes and took another bite. Legs didn't want to scare her, so he plastered on what he thought was a pleasant smile before he spoke. "Now then, what's your name?"

She ate two more forkfuls of eggs before she met his gaze. "Audrey Byrne."

"So Audrey, what is going on? Why are you here in this motel in California?"

Pain flashed across her face, and she lifted her hand to her mouth, trying to stop the sob but not having any luck. Meredith glanced over and looked like she was about to come to them, but Legs smiled, and she settled down.

"Audrey, I can't help you if you don't give me something to go on."

She met his gaze and leaned in. Her expression was fiercer than he'd seen it since she'd pointed that gun at him. "Why would you help me?"

He shrugged and took a bite of his food, watching the way she moved. Now that she had some food in her, she sat straighter and held her head higher. She'd washed her face, and some of her cracked ceramic look faded and had been replaced with something closer to relief.

"I have coffee." Legs almost laughed at the way her eyes went wide. He stood and moved to his thermos. It was a few hours old, but his thermos kept liquid hot. He'd made it for the hike he planned on taking after his shower.

She took the mug from him and lifted it to her nose, breathing in deeply. The sigh that escaped her lips made his balls pull up tight. *Down, boy*, he said to himself as he watched her sip the coffee like it was the finest elixir in all the land. She opened her eyes and met his gaze, smiling for the first time. She looked pretty, younger. When he'd first seen her, he placed her age closer to thirty-five, but now she looked like she was in her twenties.

"I'm going on a hike in a bit," Legs said. "Come with me."

Audrey's eyes went hard, and her skin pinched a little, making her look older again. But Meredith was up, bouncing around them.

"Mommy, please? I want to go out into the forest."

Audrey cupped Meredith's chin. "We don't have the shoes for it."

"Just a quick trip to the store. Come on. It will be fun."

"Please!" Meredith begged.

He could tell the moment Audrey relented. Now he had his hiking companion. It would change which trail he planned to go on, but still, he wanted the company.

A little voice in the back of his head warned him that getting involved might be messy. Audrey showed no signs of drug use, and Meredith seemed well behaved underneath the fear evident in her eyes. He wanted to help them and felt confident he could handle any problems that showed up.

CHAPTER 2

Audrey wanted to tell Tony he was foolish for spending that much money, but Meredith seemed happy. It was the first time they'd really relaxed since she'd escaped six weeks ago. She couldn't believe they'd survived this long. She thought for sure she would be dead, and Meredith would be shipped off to some expensive boarding school, or worse. That was the last thing she wanted for her daughter, a disconnected life, pawned off on wherever Eddy could send her.

Life would have been so much easier if she'd never gone out with Eddy. Sure, he was older, but not by much, and he had a wild side, but she hadn't known he was a criminal until eight months ago.

She'd suspected something bad, but she hadn't been prepared for what she'd found.

Life had been almost perfect if she ignored the weird things Eddy requested and his demeaning demands he put on her at night. She didn't mind his name calling because he didn't interfere with her raising Meredith how she saw fit. If he had, she would have left him much earlier. Her parents had approved of Eddy. That should have been her first clue to run away from him.

Then everything had changed the day she walked into the garage, the one where he said he kept his precious cars she wasn't allowed to drive. Just thinking about it made her sick. She couldn't let her daughter grow up in a house where her father murdered people in the garage. Who did that?

For six and a half long months, she'd been able to convince Eddy she wouldn't tell a soul about what she'd seen. He'd threatened to kill her and Meredith if she breathed one word. Weeks slipped by, and her fear grew as her mind tumbled over the horrific scene she'd walked in on.

Honestly, she would say anything, do anything to convince Eddy she loved him and wasn't desperately searching for a way to escape. Divorce wasn't an option. Eddy had made sure she understood what would happen if she filed for a divorce. First off, she would never see Meredith again. Second, she would end up in some brothel in South Africa or some other place where she'd never be able to escape.

Every day had been hell trying to convince Eddy she wouldn't say anything. And then she'd found the drugs tucked under Meredith's bed, stored in boxes that should have held her daughter's toys. She couldn't live with Eddy, not with the drugs in Meredith's room, add to it the murders in the garage, and it was way too much. She wouldn't put Meredith in that type of danger. It would take only one police raid, or worse, a raid from a rival gang, and her daughter would be dead.

Audrey planned their escape, waiting for the right time. She'd almost run a few times but chickened out. And then it happened. Eddy and his men were gone for the day. He'd left her alone, and she'd run. They'd left without a trace, except for her phone. Luckily, she knew how to turn off the tracking software on her phone, and she shut that down fast. But Eddy still had her number, and he'd called, vowing to kill her. He didn't want her back. No, Eddy made it abundantly clear he wanted her dead.

"We're here," Tony said as they pulled off the road

and into a dirt lot. He parked the SUV and got out, helping Meredith out of the booster seat he'd purchased. He'd spent way too much money, and Audrey prayed he didn't want anything from her. A shiver snaked down her spine, wondering what in the hell she'd gotten herself into.

"Okay, first rule, Meredith. You cannot run to anything that looks interesting. If you want to see something, you ask me, and I'll get you there and keep you safe."

Meredith nodded at Tony like he was speaking the gospel truth. Audrey stretched, breathing in the fresh air, trying to stay calm though fear raced through her like a freight train. When Eddy had taken them on vacations, they'd gone to places like Dubai or Indonesia. They'd even gone to Russia once. All Audrey had wanted was a camping trip like this.

Audrey grabbed the bag of snacks, and Tony took it from her. "I can carry that." She didn't want to sound like a petulant child, but she feared she'd come off that way.

Tony gave her another smile, making her feel warm. Eddy hadn't smiled at her like that since she'd had Meredith. "Listen, I'm sure you can, but you might need your hands free on this hike. And I don't want your weight distribution hampered by a pack."

"That doesn't make any sense. You're carrying Meredith, who, by the way, is heavy compared to the food."

The way Tony's lips pulled up as laughter spilled out made her insides wiggly. She sucked in a breath, trying to calm down. She couldn't get involved with anyone. Not that she and Eddy had love between them. Hell, it had been years since he'd said he loved her, and at least ten months, maybe more, since he'd come to her for sex. The reprieve had been nice, but she knew it meant he had sex with other women. She should have divorced him after—or maybe before Meredith had been born. Somehow, he'd convinced her to stay when they'd hit the first bump in their relationship. She'd been so naïve back then. After Meredith, Eddy had meant money and what she thought was stability. Of course, she hadn't known that Eddy was a wildcard in a very unstable structure.

"Listen, Audrey, Meredith weighs fifty pounds at most. That's nothing compared to the pack and equipment I normally carry. This will be a walk in the park compared to most days for me."

She narrowed her gaze, not believing him. "Are you sure?"

He winked as he put on the pack with Meredith in it, not even grunting as he adjusted her on his back.

"I can see forever up here," Meredith laughed as she looked around.

"How about we sing a song?" Tony asked as they took off.

"Do you know 'Twinkle, Twinkle Little Star?'" Meredith asked.

"Yes, why yes, I do."

Audrey chuckled as Tony began singing with Meredith, stopping to tell her about trees and bushes and animals as they went. When they stopped for a snack about an hour into their hike, Meredith danced around the clearing, looking happier than she had in weeks. Audrey feared she'd damaged Meredith. Seeing her daughter so happy made her believe Meredith was more resilient than she'd thought. Her daughter would get over the trauma of being jerked from her home and taken on this wild ride.

"Should we be quiet as we go on the next part of our hike?" Audrey asked.

Tony shook his head. "I don't want to sneak up

on a bear or mountain lion."

"Oh, I hadn't thought about that."

"It's a wild place out here. Dangerous."

Audrey snorted. "I keep getting myself into danger."

Tony lifted his eyebrows but said nothing as Meredith asked questions about landscape and animals. Audrey was impressed by how patient Tony was. Eddy's lack of patience with Meredith had worried Audrey. She'd hired a nanny to stay with Meredith when she needed to leave the house instead of relying on Eddy for help.

A few months after giving birth, she'd left Meredith with Eddy to take a shower instead of trying to rush her shower between naps. She'd finished the shower and found Meredith alone on the floor in her room, screaming her head off. There'd been a bruise on Meredith's back, but she didn't know if Eddy had done it. After that incident, she never asked Eddy to watch Meredith again, and he'd never volunteered.

Really, Meredith didn't know Eddy. Not like a daughter should know her father. They didn't spend time together, which was Eddy's fault. Not once since she'd taken off had Meredith said she missed her father.

Tony put Meredith into the pack, then turned to face her. Audrey's heart melted at the look on his face and how happy her daughter seemed. It was exactly the type of life she wanted for Meredith. But Audrey didn't need to get ahead of herself. Tony would be gone in a few days, and Audrey would need to find a new place to stay. Heck, she should probably bug out today. She shouldn't have gone on this hike, but Tony had been so nice, and now she was out here with her daughter, and she felt better than she had in ages.

Meredith had been asking questions nonstop since their break, and Audrey hadn't been paying attention until Meredith asked Tony where he lived.

"Right now, I'm in Hawaii. That could change, I doubt it, but I go where they send me."

"Wait, what?" Audrey asked.

Tony slowed and glanced back, his eyes full of merriment. "I'm stationed with the Navy in Hawaii. I probably won't get moved anytime soon, but it could happen. My team is solid, but we just had one member leave, and we're supposed to get someone new. I'm not sure who it will be, but we've had a few rotating members come through."

"So you're in the Navy?" Audrey couldn't believe

she'd met someone in the Navy out here in the middle of Yosemite.

"Yep. All of my adult life. It's a great job for me. I don't have to sit behind a desk. I mean, I have paperwork, but I also spend a lot of time outside doing physical activity."

"Oh, makes sense," Audrey said.

Tony's eyebrows rose as he stared at her. "What?"

"The pack with Meredith. You saying that you could handle it?"

A bird swooped low in front of them, and Meredith gasped. "What was that?"

Tony chuckled as he began talking about birds and different types. After another twenty minutes, they came to a lookout with a viewing platform with safety rails. Audrey didn't mind Meredith running around in this area. The rails would keep her safe. They rested for about twenty minutes while Meredith ran around, looking at rocks, sticks, and dirt. Before Tony put Meredith back in the pack, he bent low and waved Meredith to stand in front of him, telling her to be quiet.

"Look down there. About the middle of the valley near the creek. Do you see that?"

"What is it?" Meredith whispered.

Tony pulled out a pair of small binoculars. "A

bear. Let me see if I can help you get a look at it."

Tony's ability to answer all of Meredith's questions surprised Audrey. She'd never seen a man so willing to spend time with a child. Worry ate away at her confidence. What if he—she couldn't finish the thought. She would watch him like a hawk, but so far, he just seemed like a nice guy. But guys weren't nice, or she didn't know any who were.

Meredith watched the bear for a long moment, then the animal ran into the trees. "Oh, make it come back."

Tony chuckled as he helped Meredith into the pack. "No one can make a bear do what it doesn't want to."

Meredith looked happy on his back. After another twenty minutes, the trail turned, and they were heading back the way they'd come, or she thought so.

"Are we heading back now?"

Tony nodded. "We should be. It's a little shorter on the way back."

Audrey laughed. "How could it be shorter?"

Tony winked, and heat blossomed inside. The man was freaking gorgeous when he didn't look serious. Heck, even serious, he looked good. He did have a look that scared her. When she'd held that gun up, threatening him, he'd looked like he could have taken her head off easily. Now, he seemed so relaxed, unlike that man she'd first encountered behind the dumpster.

"The long way of the path shoots out, away from the other path. This one is a straight line back to the parking lot."

Audrey narrowed her gaze at him. "Did you memorize the map?"

"It's an easy trail with well-defined paths."

"It doesn't look well defined to me."

"Then aren't you glad you have me with you?" Tony winked again, and heat flew to her face.

This man turned her inside out. She wondered how different her life would have been if she'd met him instead of Eddy. Meredith squealed as a bunny hopped out onto the trail. Tony chuckled, then pointed out more small animals.

The man was a natural with kids. Maybe he wasn't really a nice guy and had a wife taking care of a passel of children back home. She needed to figure that out. A heavy sigh escaped her lips. She didn't have time to get to know this sweet man. Her top priority was getting away from Eddy. By the time she escaped Eddy's reach, a guy like Tony would be taken.

CHAPTER 3

They let Meredith play around the picnic tables set up close to the parking lot after they finished their hike. She still had energy, and the area was mostly safe. Tony corrected her a few times about straying too far, which Audrey liked that Tony was kind even when correcting her daughter.

Meredith sat down at one of the tables and was playing with a few sticks, rocks, and flowers while she and Tony leaned against a fence blocking off a stand of trees.

Tony met her gaze, his expression serious. "Tell me what's got you so afraid."

All the good Audrey had felt throughout their walk seemed to fade away as reality steamrolled right over her. "You don't have to take on my problems."

He shrugged, like what she might say would be easy. "It might not be a problem."

She shook her head. "It's a problem, and you shouldn't get involved."

"Why don't you let me figure out what is a problem and what isn't? I'm not—"

"God, why are men so...so—"

"Mommy," Meredith whined, drawing Audrey's attention. "Don't argue. He wants to help."

Heat swept through her. Even Meredith was ganging up against her. "Honey, let me take care of it."

"No!" Meredith shook her head so fast it made Audrey want to laugh and cry at the same time. "You can trust him."

Audrey moved to the table and sat so she was at eye level with Meredith. "We can't trust people just because they seem nice."

Tony moved close and sat next to her. "Your mother is right. Not everyone nice can be trusted."

"But you're different. I can tell." Meredith stood on the bench and stomped her foot. "You said you wouldn't allow anything to hurt me on the walk, and

I could tell by the look in your eyes. You aren't a liar."

Tony nodded. "I'll never lie to you. I'll always tell you the truth. I may not allow you to do what you want, but I'll tell you why and won't hide the truth."

"See, Mommy, he's not like Eddy. He's not a liar."

Audrey's lips thinned, and she closed her eyes. She didn't know what to do. Living with Eddy had warped her sense of truth. She'd spent so many years under his thumb, doing exactly what he asked her to do, never talking back, never disobeying, always doing his bidding, until Meredith came along. Maybe Audrey no longer knew what a good man looked like.

Tony stood. "How about we pack up and head back to the hotel? I could use a shower, then we can grab some lunch?"

"Yes, lunch," Meredith cheered.

Audrey was hungry. She guessed they'd worked up an appetite on the hike. Later, she could talk to Tony…maybe. But would telling him everything save her or get her in more trouble? If only she could trust him, then she wouldn't feel like she'd let down Meredith. She should have known better where Eddy was concerned. Of course, when she'd first met Eddy, he'd been different, nicer.

The trees were tall, preventing them from seeing too far left or right as they drove. She didn't mind. Instead, she felt like the trees protected her. As they rounded a bend and could see down into the valley where their hotel was located, they both gasped at the plume of smoke rising in the distance.

"That looks bad," Audrey said.

"What, Mommy?" Meredith shouted as she wiggled from side to side, trying to get a look.

"Something is on fire down there," Tony said.

"I wonder…" Audrey had a bad feeling about this. She prayed she was wrong, but her fears grew as they drove closer to the hotel. About two blocks away, they were met by a police officer.

"You're going to have to turn around, sir," the officer, who couldn't be older than twenty, said.

"Our hotel is that way. We just need to get to the Mountain View."

"Well, that's the problem. They've got it under control, but you aren't getting back to the Mountain View for a few hours."

Audrey gasped and looked around, searching for anyone who looked like they could be working for Eddy. She didn't see anyone watching them and relaxed a little.

Tony nodded slowly. "Great. Any idea what

started it?"

The officer shrugged. "I'm new. They don't tell me anything. I just do what I'm told."

Tony chuckled and his smile spread wide. "I totally understand. I'm military, so I follow orders, too. Good luck with your career here."

"Thank you, sir, and same to you."

Tony turned the SUV around and slowed. Meredith reached across the seat and grabbed his arm. His eyebrows raised as he cut her a glance.

"It's him. I know it is. This is too convenient."

Tony nodded and turned, driving away from the hotel. Worry crept through her. What if Tony was part of Eddy's crew, and he'd taken her away from the hotel to go hiking so someone could issue a warning? And now he was going to make her go back to Eddy?

"Where are we going?" Audrey hated the way her voice pitched high and grew tight. She didn't want to tip him off that she suspected anything.

Tony's lips were thin, and he didn't look at her. More worry filled her. She could jump out, but there's no way she would get Meredith out of his car, too.

"There's a diner on the other side of town. I don't

want to stay around here. We can eat and then figure out what we're going to do."

"I'm hungry," Meredith called out.

She was, too, but trusting Tony seemed risky. She had few choices. All of her things would have gone up in flames if she was right about the hotel. She had her purse and some money. Luckily her money was in a bank she was sure Eddy didn't know about, but otherwise, everything she had was burning in that fire back at the hotel. She wondered how her car had fared.

She reached for her neck, grasping for her necklace. It wasn't there. She'd taken it off to shower. There was no way she would get it back now. Tears filled her eyes, and she brushed them away.

Tony stopped at a stoplight and turned to stare at her, lifting his eyebrows.

Audrey shook her head. "I took off a special necklace." She blew out a breath. "At least we are alive."

Tony pulled into the diner's parking lot, which was only half full. Everyone in the restaurant seemed to be from around the area.

"You ain't local," the man behind the counter said as they walked in.

"No, sir," Tony said. "I'm stationed at Pearl Harbor and on vacation with my family."

"A Navy man," the guy behind the counter smiled so big Audrey thought his face might crack. "I was 101st Airborne during the Gulf War. Always liked the Navy, though. You guys saved my ass during another mission. Come on back. I have a quiet table with the best waitress in town."

"Thank you, sir. And thank you for your service."

"Same to you. You look bigger than the men I served with. You in Special Forces?"

Tony nodded as he slid into the seat. "Yes, sir."

"Good, good."

The guy took off, and Audrey leaned in close to him. "You told him we were family."

Tony moved closer and ducked his head. "If someone is looking for you, they'll be asking about a single woman with a girl, not a guy in the Navy from Hawaii with his family on vacation."

Audrey gasped, wondering how she'd gotten so lucky in meeting this man. He had saved her from certain death. How could she ever repay him?

The waitress came over and took their orders while joking with Meredith. Drinks were out faster than Audrey could process everything that happened this morning, and then their food was on the table.

There was too much food on her plate, and Audrey boxed up half her burger and half of Meredith's chicken tenders. Tony paid, which she wanted to argue about, but he reminded her this group thought they were a family.

After lunch, Tony headed back toward the hotel then changed directions. "What are you doing?"

"She's passed out. I figured we'd find a place in the shade and chat."

Audrey knew this was coming. She had to come up with some story to tell him, and maybe the truth was best. She'd been stupid marrying Eddy and dumb for sticking with him. She should have left before she married him. But then she wouldn't have Meredith. She loved her little girl like nothing she'd ever loved before. Her daughter had saved her sanity, and she couldn't imagine living without her.

Tony pulled over and parked at the back end of a parking lot away from the road. They both rolled down their windows and got out of the SUV, moving about ten feet away so their discussion wouldn't disturb Meredith.

Now it was truth time, and she wasn't sure how much of the truth to tell. If she told this man everything, would he go to the police?

Tony turned to face her, his expression serious. She felt like he could see right through her.

"Tell me everything, and don't leave anything out. If you do, I'll know."

Fear squeezed her chest and made her stomach clench. Based on the look on Tony's face, he would know. She swallowed over the lump in her throat, fearing his reaction when she told him about Eddy and everything he'd put them through. Surely, he would run, and then she would be left along again.

CHAPTER 4

Tony listened to her story, not reacting to the part where she talked about the dead body. He grunted at one point, and she looked up, seeing compassion on his face. After she finished, he pulled her close and held her lightly. She wasn't trapped, which she appreciated.

"You aren't disgusted by me?" Audrey whispered, fear filling her.

"No. You haven't done anything wrong."

She shook her head. "I should have gone to the cops."

Tony pushed her to arm's length. "Do you really think you could have stopped him?"

She couldn't stand staring into his eyes and let her gaze drop to the ground. "No."

"From what you said, he sounds like he tried to control you."

His words caused her chest to cave in a bit. "He did. From the day I married him."

"You will have to ask for a divorce."

Bile rose in her throat, and she had to swallow to keep it down. She wanted to deny his words, tell him that was impossible. "He's going to try to take Meredith. He knows I'll bow to him if he threatens her. She's the reason I stuck around so long."

Tony had his arms crossed over his chest, but he wasn't threatening her, not like Eddy used to. "Do you think the hotel fire was because of him?"

She nodded, her eyes still not rising to meet his. "I do."

Tony was silent for a while, so she glanced up, seeing him staring off into the distance. She shouldn't have burdened him with this. He didn't deserve the crap she brought with her. Sooner or later, Eddy would catch up with them, and he would destroy anyone who had helped her.

"I should leave." She hated how her words shook as she spoke.

Tony cocked up his eyebrows and shook his head. "Where would you go?"

"I don't know. Another town, another state. I'll find somewhere we'll fit in."

Tony grabbed her arms just above her elbows and lowered just a little so they were almost eye level. "He's going to keep looking for you. You won't be able to escape him. He'll come after you again and again. This will only stop if you confront him."

She shook her head, wanting to deny his words though she knew they were the truth. "I can't lose Meredith."

"I get that." Tony bit his lower lip, and she had to turn away so she didn't stare at him. He was too handsome, and she needed to focus on Meredith, not this man.

"If he finds me, I'm as good as dead."

"How can we keep him from finding you?"

Audrey shrugged. "I don't know. I thought I was safe. He's never going to give up."

"How about we go back to the hotel and get my stuff? Then we'll figure out a plan."

"Won't he see me, or whoever it was who set the fire?"

Tony lifted one shoulder. "It's not like I can leave you here alone with Meredith. If Eddy's man finds you, you'll be vulnerable."

She shook her head. "I'm in too big of a mess. I should have never—"

"Hey, there's no sense in beating yourself up. Let's just work toward something instead of away from it."

He was right, and she hated it. She had to confront Eddy and really leave him. But the judge would give at least half-time custody to Eddy, putting Meredith in danger. She needed to prove Eddy was a criminal, but how?

She'd seen him go in front of a judge a few times, and every single time Eddy ended up getting off free. Nothing stuck, and she doubted anything ever would. Eddy was golden. She would never beat him at any game, but Tony might.

CHAPTER 5

They stuck around the parking lot until Meredith woke. She was grumpy and wanted her stuffed animal. Legs didn't want to be the one who broke it to Meredith that her treasured stuffties were gone.

The police had cleared the area around the hotel, only allowing registered guests to return. There were four ways of getting to the hotel. Legs chose the one he'd driven earlier. Lucky for him, the young officer he'd spoken with before was still on shift, and he waved them through, not taking their information like he had the car before them.

"That was lucky," Audrey said.

"It was. I try to be nice to people, and I'm glad it worked out this time."

"The door to your unit is on the other side of the

building. Hopefully, if someone is watching the hotel, they won't see us," Audrey said.

Legs was worried, too. He'd rescued then walked away from countless people, but Audrey was different. He didn't want to turn away, leaving her to fend for herself. But he couldn't stay here in California forever. He would have to return to Hawaii in eight days. He doubted all of Audrey's problems would be solved by then.

"Oh, that looks bad," Audrey said as they drove past the front of the hotel.

He glanced at her and saw raw disappointment on her face. "Was that your room?"

"Yes, and my car. It looks like our room was smack dab in the middle of the fire."

"Dang, that's awful." Worry ate at Legs. She was left without a vehicle, her clothes, everything. She needed real help. He might be able to call in a few favors, but she needed something more than just a place to crash for a few nights.

Legs parked the vehicle on the other side of the building, away from the fire. Before getting out, he glanced around, not seeing anyone. "It looks clear."

Audrey nodded and opened her door. She slid out and headed to the door while Legs grabbed

Meredith. Once inside the room, they both breathed a little easier.

"You need to use the restroom," Audrey said to Meredith as they walked into the hotel room.

"No, I don't," Meredith countered like only a four-year-old could.

Legs frowned, not wanting to get in the middle of their argument, but he wanted to side with Audrey. It had been a while, and Meredith had just woken up. Kids peed when fully dressed sometimes, and they didn't have time to deal with messy pants. Also, all of Meredith's clothes had gone up in flames. There wasn't anything for her to change into. They needed to solve that, but not here in this town. They needed to get away, and they could stop at the next town where he would feel safer.

He cleared his throat, and both Meredith and Audrey looked at him. "Would you please use the restroom while we pack up? I need to use the bathroom, too, and I'm sure your mother will."

Meredith's lips pressed together. "Only 'cause you asked nice." Meredith traipsed off to the bathroom, and Audrey rolled her eyes.

Legs smiled and winked as he thought of all the times he'd given his parents hell. They'd been good people, but he'd been obstinate as a mule with an attitude. He didn't see them as much as he used to, but then again, his dad was angry he'd joined the Navy instead of the Air Force. That Legs had become a SEAL only made it worse.

"Can I help you pack?"

"You can grab the food. Whatever hotel we pick next will need to have a kitchenette."

Audrey raised her eyebrows. "Next."

He met her gaze. "I'm not dropping you off. Not until I know no one is after you."

Meredith wandered out from the bathroom. "I couldn't wash my hands."

Audrey's lips turned down then she grabbed her bag and pulled out a tube of sanitizer, helping Meredith clean her hands before she grabbed a towel and wiped them.

Legs shoved his clothes into his suitcase and glanced around, making sure he had everything.

A knock at his door interrupted him. He waved for Meredith and Audrey to head into the bathroom. Meredith looked like she was about to complain when Audrey whispered something to her.

Legs checked the peephole, seeing the woman who worked the front desk. "We're giving everyone a refund for the days they already paid for but didn't use."

"What about the people who were in the burned-out unit?"

The woman shrugged. "Refund plus a hundred dollars. They can take up any claims with our insurance."

Audrey stepped out of the bathroom, and the woman narrowed her gaze. "Ain't you from one of those burned-out units?"

"Yes, ma'am. I'm Amy."

"That's right. Saw someone fire something into your unit. You're lucky you weren't there. You'd be dead."

Legs didn't miss the shiver nor how pale Audrey turned. She took the money from the clerk but didn't ask how to get the insurance reimbursement. He guessed Audrey didn't want to deal with the hassle. He didn't blame her. It would be difficult to come back and get money if she was trying to hide.

"Sorry about this. No electricity, no water. I guess we'll be shut down for a while." The woman turned and walked off.

Legs checked outside, making sure no one watched. The area seemed clear. He shut the door and handed Audrey the money from his refund.

"I can't take this," Audrey said.

"You need money to stay afloat."

"We'll be fine. I have some cash that should last us for a few more months."

"You need years."

A shiver snaked through her. "Hopefully, we can move somewhere and settle down."

"Listen, I'm—"

"Why won't the TV work?" Meredith whined.

They both turned to look at her pointing the remote at the TV and clicking the button.

"Sorry, honey, no power. It's the same reason the lights don't work," Audrey said.

Meredith turned to them and frowned. "I don't like it."

"We're headed to another hotel. One with a TV," Legs said.

Meredith's eyes went wide, and her lips curved up in a smile. "We're staying with you?"

"Sure are," Legs said. Audrey frowned at him, and he shrugged. "You need a place to stay."

"Fine, but I can pay for my own—"

Legs shook his head. "Just accept my help. It will make it easier in the end."

Audrey rolled her eyes again, and Legs decided he liked her attitude. She wasn't a pushover, and he bet if they were on more equal footing, she would give him hell.

They loaded the SUV, and he strapped Meredith in while Audrey made sure the door had closed all the way. They were pulling out of the lot when something slammed into the side panel of the SUV. He knew that sound like he knew his own face. Someone was firing on them.

CHAPTER 6

Audrey screamed as Tony punched the accelerator. Fear for Meredith filled her as she scrambled out of her seatbelt and moved to the backseat, pulling Meredith low. Meredith hadn't known what was going on, but the fear in her eyes showed she didn't like it.

The vehicle turned a corner, and Tony slammed on the brakes then got out. Audrey held Meredith down, praying Tony knew what he was doing.

She heard people talking and then more noise. Then she heard multiple shots. Both her and Meredith were crying as they lay in a heap in the back of the SUV.

Suddenly the shooting stopped, and she could hear more voices. Then the door on the passenger side opened. She looked up, seeing worry all over Tony's face.

"Are you two okay?"

Audrey nodded, but Meredith voiced her anger. "Mommy is crushing me."

Tony helped her up and grabbed Meredith, checking her over to make sure she really was fine. It made her heart squeeze that Tony was that worried about her daughter.

"W-what happened?" Audrey got out.

"Don't know, but the man won't be shooting anyone else ever again," Tony said.

Audrey narrowed her gaze. "What do you mean?"

Tony angled his head toward Meredith, then gave his head a slow shake. He didn't want to talk about it in front of her daughter. That meant the guy must be dead.

An officer approached their vehicle, his eyes wide. "Sorry about that. We don't get this much excitement here ever. I have no idea why he was shooting at you."

Tony shrugged. "Who knows? Maybe he was a vagrant or just someone up from LA on drugs. We see it in our area from time to time. And he could have just been firing his gun, not really caring what he shot."

"Well, we're so sorry for your trouble. We'll let you and your wife get on. I have your number if I need to contact you. It looks like you were just in the wrong place at the wrong time. I'm glad nothing happened to your sweet family."

Tony nodded, and Audrey strapped Meredith back into her seat. She didn't like that another person thought she and Tony were married. But the story did hide the truth of who she was. That guy wasn't just shooting wildly. He was aiming at her. She could have easily been killed along with Meredith. Eddy was trying to eliminate her.

They were lucky the cops didn't want them to stick around and take their names. She sighed as they drove away from the hotel and the cops, heading north. After twenty minutes, Tony turned to the east. They drove for a little over an hour, then stopped for a snack and restroom break before heading east again. It was close to seven that evening when they stopped at a hotel. Audrey had no clue where they were, but they weren't in the same city, and it would be difficult for Eddy to track her here.

"I'll go in and get a room. No need for you two to be on the video if they have cameras," Tony said.

Audrey closed her eyes and blew out a breath, wishing she could give Meredith a stable environment. Soon she would be old enough to start school, and Meredith would need a secure place to call home. They'd need to live in the same town for at least a while. Hopping from school to school would surely ruin Meredith's future. Why wasn't hiding from Eddy as easy as they made it seem in movies? She just needed to find a town where they could hide in plain sight.

Guilt slid through her. She'd called her mother for her birthday. That's the only reason she could come up with why Eddy had found her. It had been shortsightedness calling her mom, but she was just trying to be a good daughter. Audrey had wondered, but now she knew her parents didn't care about her happiness or safety. Her mom had to have told Eddy they were in California.

"Is that a dinosaur?" Meredith asked.

Maybe it will eat us, and this will all be over. Audrey pushed the thought away and opened her eyes. "Where?" Audrey turned to look at Meredith, who pointed out the window. She followed where her daughter was looking and blinked at the figure. The sun was gone, but there was still enough glow so it wasn't pitch black outside.

"It won't move, will it?" Meredith's voice shook.

"No, honey, it's not real. I think it's a dinosaur statue."

"Why would that be here?"

Audrey settled in her seat and closed her eyes. "Maybe they found dinosaur bones around here."

"Do you think we'll see one?"

Audrey shook her head. "Bones, yes. A live one, no. It's not like the movies. They haven't brought any of them back." Anger whipped through Audrey. Eddy had thought it was funny to have Meredith watch *Jurassic Park*. She'd gone out to shop, and the nanny had been in charge. Eddy had snuck upstairs and put *Jurassic Park* on for Meredith when the nanny had gone downstairs to get breakfast. Her daughter had been traumatized. Eddy thought it had been hilarious to see Meredith afraid.

Tony stepped out of the office and his lips curved up. He opened the driver's side door and slid in. "We're at the back, away from the noise. We've got a suite."

Audrey's mouth fell open. "A as in one?"

Tony didn't look at her as he nodded. "I'll sleep on the couch."

Meredith started talking a mile a minute about dinosaurs, and Audrey didn't have the energy to argue with Tony about the room. What was it to her if he wanted to sleep on the couch?

They stumbled into the room, and Audrey dropped to the couch. Tony held up his phone and raised his eyebrows.

"Pizza?"

She nodded, and Meredith jumped around, looking way too excited for a child who needed to be in bed in an hour or so. She'd tried her best to keep up with a routine. Of course, it had been difficult. They'd survived, which they wouldn't have done if Tony hadn't shown up. She was grateful for him but not grateful enough for sex. She hoped he didn't want that.

The room was nice. It had a living space separated from the sleeping room with an actual door. The kitchenette table had four chairs, and the refrigerator was full-sized.

Audrey knew she needed to get her shit together and stood. "Thank you for the room. This will be a good place to start."

"Let's get some food in us, and then you and I can discuss your options later."

Meredith was happy they had a working TV. The food arrived, and by the time Meredith had eaten one slice, she looked exhausted. Audrey had to insist she take a bath, which Meredith voiced rather loudly she didn't want to. By eight forty-five, Audrey was back in the main room, and Meredith was asleep.

Audrey dropped to the couch and groaned. Tony turned to look at her, and she had to close her eyes so she didn't turn to him and stare at his face that was becoming more and more good-looking to her. Maybe it was gratitude doing the talking in her head, making her think he was hot.

"I know some people who could get you hooked up with a women's shelter."

She shook her head and glanced at Tony, seeing concern shining in his eyes. She was glad he wasn't looking at her with lust. "I don't want to be a shelter woman. And you saw what happened to the motel. If he ever found out I was in a shelter, all the women there would be dead."

Tony nodded and stood, moving to the kitchen where he grabbed a package of cookies from the bags they'd grabbed before running from the burned-out hotel. He offered her the package, but she waved it off. She was already eating terribly, and she didn't need to add cookies to the list of guilts.

"What do you think your options are?" Tony asked.

She stared at him, trying to gauge if he was being

an ass or helpful. He wasn't smirking and looked concerned. She decided he wasn't being a jerk. "I don't know. Were you asking that so you could tell me how wrong I was and then explain what I should do?"

He held up his hand and shook his head. "No. I just deal with a lot of people in bad situations."

She narrowed her eyes as she stared at him. "Wait, what do you do with the Navy?"

He shook his head and waved his hand like he was shooing the question away. "That's not important. What is important is what you want to do and how you're going to get it to happen."

"I want Eddy to leave me alone. I just want Meredith to be able to grow up without drama. That's not possible now. I married a psychopath, and now I'm paying for it." Tears spilled from her eyes.

It took Tony a moment before he moved close with a box of tissues. His arm draped over her shoulder, and her shoulders rolled inward with the weight of his arm and all the emotions running through her. She needed to make one thing clear to him.

"I can't have sex with you."

Tony backed off, his hands raised. "Whoa. I'm not

asking for sex. I really just want you two to be settled."

"Do you have a wife or girlfriend back in Hawaii?"

He shook his head. "No."

"How are you so good with Meredith then?" He shrugged, not answering the question. "Are you some kind of pervert looking to take advantage of a woman with a kid? I'll tell you right now, I'll gut you in your sleep if you touch my daughter."

Tony seemed to calm to an almost eerie level. "I'm not looking to take advantage of you. Two weeks ago, right before leave, I was in another country, helping a woman hold a cloth over her child's chest, knowing the kid was already dead. But holding that cloth over his chest kept the woman from screaming. I've seen the worst of the worst. Children Meredith's age in brothels being used by sex traffickers. I've seen women and children desperate enough to do anything. I know how depraved life can be. I can't accept that here in the USA. I don't risk my life so that kind of shit can happen here."

Audrey blinked at him, unsure what to say. She'd been so involved in her own life she hadn't stopped to think how others had it. "I'm sorry."

"You don't have to be sorry. I just want to help if I can. I know a few people who can get you a place at a good women's shelter, but I understand your hesitancy."

Audrey closed her eyes and rubbed her forehead. Pain slithered down her back, and she moaned.

"We don't have to figure it out tonight. Why don't you go shower and get some sleep?"

Guilt slid through Audrey. "There are two queen beds in there. I'll sleep with Meredith, and you can take the other bed."

Tony held up his hands. "I don't want you—"

"I insist. Besides, this couch is too small, and it looks like crap. Just take the other bed, and then we'll all get a good night's sleep. Tomorrow we can discuss plans."

Tony didn't look like he wanted to agree at first, then he gave a sharp nod. "But if you feel uncomfortable, I'll sleep out here."

He was too nice of a guy. She didn't know if there was anything else lurking under the surface, but she knew no men like him. Other guys would be chatting her up, trying to get her to at least suck their dicks, but this man was being nice. It made her worry, but then that made her wonder why she knew so many terrible men. Maybe this was what regular people were like, or was this guy some sort of superhero?

Tony had saved her, that was for sure. She needed time and a miracle. Maybe Tony was part of the miracle that would save her.

CHAPTER 7

Legs woke to Meredith crawling into his bed. He let go of the breath he'd sucked in when he'd felt the bed move. It hadn't taken him more than half a second to remember he was in a room with Audrey and Meredith. He was glad he hadn't lashed out.

"I'm hungry," Meredith said.

"Go use the bathroom, and I'll see what I can get you for breakfast."

She climbed off the bed and headed to the bathroom. He sat up and met Audrey's gaze.

"I don't know why she bothered you instead of asking me."

Tony shrugged as he made his way to the bathroom that Meredith had just finished using. He brushed his teeth, demanding his dick fall in line and go soft.

Audrey didn't need some stupid guy falling all over her. She needed someone to help. He wouldn't be the kind of jerk who took advantage of women who were down.

He joined Meredith in the main room, looking at the food that had survived. There wasn't much for breakfast.

"Let's get your shoes on and go grab something from McDonald's. I saw one about a mile away when we were pulling in last night."

"Yea!" Meredith cheered.

He really liked her enthusiasm. While Meredith was pulling on her shoes, he called into the bedroom, "We're headed to get breakfast. What would you like?"

Audrey popped open the bathroom door. "Give me a minute, and I'll come with you."

"Sure." He told himself he wasn't excited that Audrey wanted to go with him. They weren't in a relationship, and that wouldn't change. Audrey only wanted help, not him hitting on her.

It turned out to be a good thing Audrey came with him because there was a play structure inside, and Meredith wanted to explore it.

Audrey sat across from him at a table. She looked good, and he wanted to do more than just talk.

Hitting on her was out of the question. She didn't need another idiot in her life.

No one else was in the playroom, so he had time to discuss the situation with Audrey. "Do you feel better this morning?" Tony asked.

She shrugged. "I don't know. We were shot at yesterday."

Tony nodded. "We were. He seems pretty serious about punishing you."

She took a sip of her coffee which was more like a dessert, but he wouldn't say anything about her drinking a super sweet coffee the day after being shot at. Few people knew what that felt like, and it screwed with their minds. She hadn't fallen apart, and he was thankful for that.

"I just want a place where I can be safe."

Tony pressed his lips thin. He'd had a thought earlier, one that he shouldn't be having, of her with him, living together in Hawaii. Maybe he should call Tex or one of the other retired guys he knew and ask them for the location of a shelter on this side of the country. He could drive Audrey and Meredith to the location and get them settled. Those places had resources, and then he could walk away and finish off his leave by the beach, soaking in some rays, which was exactly what he hadn't wanted to do in Hawaii and why he'd left.

He met Audrey's gaze, and the question was out of his mouth before he could stop himself. "Come to Hawaii. I have a three-bedroom house."

She blinked at him, and then her mouth fell open. Meredith circled around and grabbed another bite of food, and drank some water before she took off into the play structure.

"Hawaii?"

"Do you think he has anyone watching the airlines, like the FBI or something?"

Audrey shook her head. "No way he would invite the FBI or any other government agency into his house. They'd have a field day being given access to that place. Could you imagine how much trouble he would be in? He—" Audrey looked around, then leaned in close across the table. "He killed someone in our garage. I'm sure that wasn't the first person he murdered there. The cops probably already suspect he's done some awful stuff, but they haven't been invited inside. If he called in the cops, they would gather evidence against him, and he would be in jail."

"So you could fly and—"

"What about the tickets?" Audrey stopped speaking when Meredith ran over and whispered something in her ear. "Sorry, we'll be back in a moment."

Tony watched them until they were in the bathroom. He shouldn't have suggested she come to Hawaii. What was he doing? She obviously wasn't interested in him, but that didn't matter. He didn't care about that. He just wanted to help. He could help her find a job, get Meredith into school, and then what? What would happen if he dated someone? He wouldn't kick Audrey and Meredith out. But no girlfriend would allow him to keep living with Audrey. Maybe he didn't need a girlfriend. He hadn't so far. He could do this. Now he only needed to believe it and not ruin Audrey and Meredith's life by trying to save them.

CHAPTER 8

They weren't traveling together, but Audrey was amazed Tony had found them flights on another airline that landed at about the same time as his return flight to Hawaii.

They'd spent two days hiking Yosemite, then they'd traveled to LA and spent a few days sightseeing. Meredith was having fun with Tony, which made her heart sing.

Audrey didn't like the way her feelings had changed for Tony. She couldn't pursue anything. It wouldn't be right. Besides, Tony had made it clear he was doing this out of the goodness of his heart, not because he found her attractive.

She was a mess. Running from Eddy had aged her. She'd stopped taking care of herself. It was hard to get a salon appointment while running from her psycho ex—almost ex. Maybe in Hawaii, her life would be calmer.

"You ready to go?" Tony asked as he stepped back into the room.

Their suitcases were loaded, and they had a little over three hours before their plane took off.

"Yes, I think we are."

"Will we live with Mr. Tony?" Meredith asked for the tenth time.

"Yes, we will live at Mr. Tony's house for a while. Until we find one of our own."

"I like him. I don't think we should move to another house."

Audrey had nothing to say about that. She liked Tony, too, but she knew he wouldn't want her around forever. Surely, he had a girlfriend or maybe multiple girls coming around, sleeping in his bed. That thought pissed her off. She shouldn't be angry. He was a good-looking guy, and there was no way he wouldn't go searching for sex.

The thought of Tony being sweaty from sex, his body stretched out over some woman, pissed her off, and sent a shiver through her. She needed to stop thinking about him naked. The other day he'd come out of the bathroom without his shirt on. That had been enough to make every inch of her body feel like fire.

They returned the car and made their way to the terminal. Her nerves were on edge. A part of her feared being stopped as they passed through security. Maybe Eddy had told the FBI about her running away with Meredith. Would they be waiting for her? But no, he couldn't have. He wouldn't want the feds looking that deeply into his business.

Nothing happened other than one of the agents telling Meredith a knock-knock joke. Audrey breathed a sigh of relief as they made their way from the checkpoint.

"Let's get some food," Tony said. "The flight will be about five or six hours long."

"We should get some snacks, too," Audrey said.

"I want a candy bar," Meredith called out as she started to take off to the shop across the way.

Tony grabbed her before she was almost run over by one of the carts. "Watch out, little one. There are too many people here."

Meredith's lower lip stuck out like she was about to cry. Audrey wanted to yell at her, but Tony was staying incredibly calm. If she blew a gasket, she'd look like a fool.

"How about we get a small candy bar that you and I can split?" Tony asked.

"I want a big one," Meredith pouted.

Tony put Meredith down and raised his eyebrows. "We can all share a big one. Your tummy is too small for a large one on your own. You might be able to eat it, but you'd feel miserable. Which one do you want to split?"

Audrey liked that he wasn't mean, but he wasn't giving into everything Meredith wanted. He'd gotten her to drink water instead of juice, he'd somehow convinced her to finish her vegetables instead of eating only bread, and she'd gone to sleep so well each night after he lifted his eyebrows and told her sleep was necessary when she'd been pitching a fit at Audrey's insistence to get some sleep.

This trip to the airport was the best she'd ever experienced though it was LAX. Meredith stayed calm, Tony made everything easier, and by the time Audrey dropped into her seat on the plane, she didn't feel like she needed a nap.

Tony's plane had loaded far away from hers, but he'd made sure she was in the proper place, that she and Meredith had gone to the restroom and had plenty of snacks. He'd been kind and hugged

Meredith goodbye before heading over to his gate. The man was too good for her.

She texted him on the burner phone he'd insisted she have.

In seat. How about you?

His text came back moments later.

I'm in my seat and ready to go.

I'll see you in a few hours.

She put her phone on do not disturb and found a movie for Meredith to watch. It wouldn't keep her entertained throughout the flight, but it would help.

Meredith was entranced with the plane and how big it was. The lady next to Meredith was kind, talking to her for about twenty minutes.

Once they were in the air, Meredith asked about the movie. Audrey relaxed and may have even slept for a bit. Though the flight was long, it didn't seem like it took too long.

She spied Tony waiting for her and Meredith when she stepped into the terminal. Her heart squeezed, and she had to force herself not to run over and hug him. Meredith jumped into his arms, looking thrilled to see him.

He insisted Meredith use the restroom because it would take them a while to get to his place. He'd taken a hired car to get to the airport, so they had to wait for someone to pick them up.

The drive wasn't too long, and they were pulling up in front of a house in what looked like a quiet neighborhood. Tony led them inside, looking nervous. She wondered why.

"So the third bedroom isn't big, but I figured Meredith didn't need a huge bed. I had friends deliver a mattress for in there, so you have your own bed, Meredith."

Meredith pursed her lips and begged to be picked up by Tony. "Can't I sleep in your room?" She played with the collar of his shirt then leaned her head on his shoulder.

Audrey glanced at her watch. It was way past her bedtime in the States but too early for her to go to bed here. She had no idea how long it would take them to adjust. They'd lived in New York before they'd run, and now they were in Hawaii. It was the middle of the night for Eddy. A shiver snaked through her, and Tony raised his eyebrows before turning down the hall and carrying Meredith to the small room.

The size wasn't so small. The bed was in one corner, and she had about six, maybe seven feet to the other wall. The closet was large for such a small room, though.

"We can decorate it this weekend," Tony said.

Meredith nodded and wiggled her way out of Tony's arms. She crawled up on the bed and looked out the window. "Is that the ocean?"

Tony nodded. "Yes. You can see the ocean from here."

She turned to him, her eyes pleading. "Can we go to the beach?"

"Not tonight. But we can go this weekend. I have work tomorrow, and we'll need to figure out transportation for you two, but for now, we need to unpack and wash clothes."

"I hate washing clothes," Meredith said. "Those places are smelly."

"Well, I have a washer and dryer here. So you

don't have to go anywhere. We can start a load and then go outside and sit on the back porch."

Meredith yawned and nodded. "I'm hungry."

"Well, I have eggs and waffles," Tony said.

"I'll make dinner if you want to wash your clothes. I can wash ours tomorrow. Meredith and I can spend the day in the neighborhood."

"There's a park about ten minutes from here. The weather should be good. I have bottles of sunscreen in every bathroom."

"That's great," Audrey said.

"We'll talk later."

Audrey nodded, wondering how the heck she would ever pay this man back. She had a stable base to raise Meredith. This was the break she'd been waiting for.

Tony showed her to a room he obviously used as his guest room. It had a full bed decorated with a colorful quilt. The photos and frames complemented the bedding well. They were a solid color that matched the yellow in the quilt. Overall, the space was happy and nice.

Once they were seated outside with their breakfast for dinner, she asked him about the room.

"Jenna and Ashley decorated it for me. Jenna is married to Vine, and Ashley is married to Wig. I gave them a budget, and they bought some great stuff."

"Wow. So are they members of your team?"

"Yes. They're the best."

Meredith got up and ran to the end of the yard, looking at his fruit trees.

Audrey watched her as she talked with Tony. "What do you think they're going to say about me?"

"They're excited to get to know you. The women aren't coming over tomorrow, but they'd like to meet you this weekend."

She whipped her head around, seeing him flash her a huge smile. "They already know?"

He nodded. "Yes. I sent a note to the group the day I met you. They're good people."

"So they know about everything?"

"No. I didn't tell them everything. I Just said I met you and that you're coming here to stay for a while. It's up to you what you tell."

Worry filled her. What if they didn't like her? Would they think she brought too much danger? Her life was a mess. She just hoped they didn't tell Tony to kick her out. Because if she was forced to leave here, she had no clue where she would end up.

CHAPTER 9

The first day back at work was always a kick in the seat of the pants. They were hit with a meeting about a terrorist group making a move on another group. Their team wasn't going in this time, but they would need to provide support for Mustang's team.

Mustang and Aleck were up, looking closely at one of the maps on the screen. Mustang shook his head. "I don't like the approach you all want us to make. We're vulnerable."

"It's a huge risk. We need to figure out a different way in," Aleck said.

Dallas Creed stood with them, his eyes narrow as he stared at the area Mustang and Aleck were talking about. "I see what you mean, but any other way is just as risky."

"Can we take a few hours and study this more?" Mustang asked.

"Yes, you're not wheels up until two in the morning."

"Thank you," Mustang said.

Midas leaned across the table and tapped the space right in front of Legs. "You're good with this stuff. Go talk to Aleck and Mustang."

Legs nodded and gave Midas a thumbs up. He was good at figuring out the terrain. They had a few hours to get this nailed down.

He moved to sit with Mustang and Aleck, searching through every photo they had of the area. The first approach would leave the guys open for too long. If the enemy caught sight of them, they could be massacred.

Every suggestion Aleck made, Mustang countered and vice versa. Legs made a comment, and they all rejected it before it even hit the floor.

"This sucks," Aleck said after about two hours.

"Tell me about it," Mustang said.

"Coffee?" Legs said as he stood.

"I'm going to hit the head, but I'd take a coffee." Aleck stood and headed out of the room.

"I heard you picked up a guest on your vacation," Mustang said.

Legs glanced at him, seeing concern. "I know it's weird. I can't explain why I thought it necessary to bring her here."

"She's on the up and up, though, right? Like you don't think she's out to scam you?"

Legs shook his head. "No. I did some searching on the internet. Once I decided to have her come here, I texted Tex. Her husband is a piece of shit, but she's just a trusting woman who was caught in the crossfire of a bad decision."

"Do you like her?" Mustang raised his eyebrows and his lips twisted to one side.

Legs blew out a breath. "She's still married. I didn't bring her over here to make her my wife. I really just want to help her."

"But she's hot, right?"

Legs rolled his eyes. "I'm not focusing on that. I want to make sure she's safe. That's my priority."

"God, you're too nice," Mustang said as he headed out of the room to the restroom.

Aleck stepped in, his expression serious. "So you have a woman and a kid living with you."

Legs chuckled as he handed Midas a cup of coffee. "Jesus, does the whole base know?"

Aleck winked. "Maybe."

"Maybe I'm stupid or too soft."

"I know you aren't soft. If you need anything..."

Legs nodded as he took a sip of his coffee. Maybe he'd bit off too much. He liked Audrey, but she wasn't available. Maybe her marriage had been over for years, but he wouldn't move forward on that front until she divorced the jerk. He would be her friend because everyone needed friends they could count on.

It was almost four that afternoon before Legs found the answer to their problem. Mustang and Aleck had gone home to say goodbye to their families and would be back by midnight. Legs shot off a note to Mustang, giving basic details. Before he left for the day, he broke down the path for Creed and the rest of the men. Mustang walked in before he ended the session.

"You're back," Legs said.

"Elodie knows how this goes. She encouraged me to return when I got your text."

Legs nodded and moved to show Mustang exactly what he'd found. After finishing his spiel, Mustang stared at the map, and the photos Legs had found. He had one arm tucked across his chest as he chewed on his thumbnail, his mind obviously spinning.

"Okay. I think that will work. We'll go over it on the flight over. I'll keep you updated."

"Be safe and kick ass," Legs said.

"We plan on it," Mustang said.

Exhausted, Legs didn't know what they would do about dinner, but he would have to figure something out. He'd texted Audrey before he'd left base. They hadn't worked out since he'd spent the day in the conference room trying to figure out the strategy Mustang's team needed to take. Not working out meant soreness had crept in. He would have to find some time, maybe after Meredith went to bed, to do some weightlifting.

Legs opened the door, and the scent of roasted meat and something else hit him. He groaned. Then Meredith was flying down the short hall and into his arms.

"We saw a huge bird today."

Her grin made his heart squeeze. Her enthusiasm was infectious, and he kissed her on the cheek before setting her on the floor to run back to her mother. Audrey stood by the couch, grinning at them both. His heart squeezed again. He hadn't brought her here to hit on her. He was her friend, that was all.

"Whatever you cooked smells delicious."

"I thought it was the least I could do. I dug through your freezer. I hope you don't mind."

"Not at all. Let me change into civis."

"Sure." Audrey laughed, looking like she had no clue what he was talking about. She probably wasn't used to military lingo. He'd have to give her a hint if he spoke about something weird. Civis she could figure out.

After changing into shorts and a T-shirt, he stepped into the kitchen and thought the food smelled even better now.

"There might be leftovers we can eat for lunch tomorrow. I was looking into schools, and there's one not that far. They have a great preschool program Meredith can go do."

"Wow, you were busy," Legs said.

"I want to be able to pay for stuff like food. You're being very nice, and I don't want to take advantage of you."

He met her gaze, wishing they were closer because if he was dating her, he would have leaned in and brushed his lips over hers or maybe cupped her cheek. "I don't think you are taking advantage of me. Now then, why don't you tell me about your day, Meredith."

Meredith talked while she ate, telling him about

the dogs they met, the equipment she played on, the pond with the birds, and the neighbor next door who was nosy. He liked hearing her excitement.

After dinner, Legs cleaned the dishes and wiped down the kitchen while Audrey played with Meredith. They took a short walk because Meredith wanted to show him the pond. Halfway home, she got tired, so he picked her up and carried her. Audrey said he didn't have to, but he didn't mind. It was nice having them with him.

He worked out in the shed housing his weights behind his house while Audrey gave Meredith a bath and put her to bed. He was almost done with his last set of exercises when Audrey came out and sat on the porch. He was aware enough to admit having her as an audience made him puff up and do more work.

Once he was done, he put up his weights. Audrey came close, carrying two glasses of water. He took one and drank about half.

"Thank you."

"If we're ever too much of a burden—"

He set the glass on a table by the shed. "You won't be."

"I just…"

Legs frowned at her as he closed the shed and locked it. He had too much equipment to risk it being stolen. "Don't worry about it. By the way, that food was amazing. Where did you learn to cook like that?"

"Oh." Audrey frowned, and the light went out of her eyes. He hadn't wanted to upset her and didn't think complimenting her cooking would, but obviously, something he said had dampened her mood.

"You don't—"

"No, it's okay. It's part of it all. Before I got married, my parents forced me to go to cooking school."

"Cooking school? Are you a trained chef?" Legs grabbed his glass of water.

Audrey rolled her eyes, and he wanted to pull her close and what...hug her...kiss her? He shoved that thought from his mind and moved to the chairs on the patio, wanting to hear the rest of her story.

They settled in the comfortable seats that circled his firepit one of the previous renters had put in. He never used it but hadn't pulled it out because the workmanship was amazing.

"So, what's the full story?"

Audrey got a far-off look on her face. "I kind of enjoyed culinary school, but I couldn't let my parents know. It was a weird time. I was forced to learn how to cook for Eddy because he needed a wife who could impress others. So I went to class and graduated close to the top. I think I was number three in the class. I love making gourmet meals. I mean, some of the ingredients needed are very expensive, but I know how to whip up some really cool stuff."

"I need to introduce you to Elodie."

"Who is that?" Audrey narrowed her gaze, and a frown turned down the corners of her mouth.

He couldn't help the smile tugging at his lips. "She's the wife of a guy I work with. She's a chef."

Audrey's shoulders curled in, and her forehead wrinkled as her eyebrows pinched together. "Oh."

He was confused. She'd said she loved making cool food. "What's wrong?"

Audrey shook her head. "Nothing. I'm just being silly. I'm embarrassed because I never worked professionally. I doubt I could. I finished school almost seven years ago and never even tried for a job."

"That doesn't mean you don't have the skills."

Audrey snorted out a laugh. "Want to know what the funniest part was?"

"What?"

"My parents sent me to culinary school to

impress Eddy, but he hated all that amazing food I could make. He liked ramen noodles, and not the really good stuff, but the packaged stuff that you add hot water to, and that's it. He didn't want anything else in there. No sauteed vegetables or meats that I could prepare and serve the dish in a five-star restaurant. Nope, just the noodles boiled, and the flavoring package dropped in and stirred."

"I'm sorry your skills weren't put to use. Did you go to the store for anything for tonight's meal?"

She shook her head, and her eyes brightened. He liked this look on her, her eyes bright, the slight smile curving up her lips. She looked even younger here in Hawaii. The fresh air and lack of stress were doing good things for her.

"No. I mean, I had to manipulate a few ingredients to make it work, but it wasn't hard."

"How long did it take you to prepare it?"

"That's hard to judge. I started pulling together ingredients as soon as you left, but Meredith wanted to go do stuff, so I worked between playing with her. I enjoyed it, though. It was fun thinking of ways to make your food work to prepare you dinner."

"I have to say that was one of the best meals I've ever had, and I've had Elodie's cooking. You are good at what you do. Don't discount your skills."

Audrey's cheeks turned pink, and she ducked her head. "Thank you."

"You know, you could get a job easily with your skills."

Audrey shook her head. "Chefs have long hours, and I have Meredith. She comes first."

"Well, you could do something like gourmet meals for people at home or something."

A worried look crossed her face. "I'm afraid he'll find me if I start working on something like that. The people who order specialty meals expect the owner to put their face on the website. I can't have my face out there. You saw what he did at that motel."

Legs sat back, staring out at the view he had of the ocean. The house was on a hill, and the neighbors behind him sat lower on the hillside. The view had sold him, that and the fact the house had been cheap because it had been partially gutted and belonged to a relative. They were renting the place to him so cheap he almost felt guilty. But he had spent the first six months fixing everything, making the place livable. He loved his house, loved how it looked now, loved everything about it. The view was visible from his bedroom, which sat on the opposite side of the house from the other two rooms. The small room Meredith slept in was on the side of the house and had a view of the ocean. The bigger bedroom where Audrey would sleep sat at the back of the house and had an impressive view, too.

This spot was his thinking spot. When his contract with the Navy had come up, he'd sat out here contemplating going private. He knew some people who knew some people in Virginia who could help him with a job, but ultimately, he'd decided to re-up with the Navy. Now he was in until retirement. Unless something came up.

"I'm not going to tell you how to feel. What happened at that hotel was scary." Legs considered himself lucky that he hadn't killed the man Eddy had sent after them. The police had taken that shot, and he'd been ever so thankful they'd done the dirty work. The number of questions he would have had to answer scared him. This way, Audrey had been free to escape with no record of their names in the official report. Hopefully, Eddy wouldn't look too deeply into what had happened. He prayed the shooter hadn't been able to pop off a text to Eddy because the last thing Audrey needed was Eddy sending another jerk after her.

CHAPTER 10

Audrey rolled over, seeing it was still before six in the morning. She had no clue what she wanted to do. She enjoyed cooking, but would working in a professional kitchen kill her joy? She didn't want to end up hating life, but she also needed work. She was good with food, but could she take the stress?

She'd actually never really held a job. Sure, she'd babysat, and she'd helped out at church events, but a real job making money had never been in the cards for her. First, it had been her parents, then Eddy, then she'd had Meredith. Time had gotten away from her, and she'd never insisted she be allowed to work. Of course, now she knew she couldn't have insisted because Eddy wasn't a reasonable person.

She got up, used the restroom, and brushed her

teeth. When she opened the bathroom door, she was shocked to see Tony already up and dressed. He sipped his coffee and sighed. He must have heard her and turned to stare down the hall. She stepped out, feeling like she was interrupting his morning.

"Good morning," she said in a near whisper, not wanting to wake Meredith.

"Did you sleep well?"

She snorted out a laugh. "I have slept so much better since I've met you than I have for the last year. Thank you."

His lips quirked up. "So I'm not heading out of the country this time, but we have some stuff going down, and I can't talk about it, but I just wanted you to know I may be really late tonight. Like I may not actually come home tonight. I'll text you if I can, but sometimes we're locked in a room and don't have access to our phones."

Audrey's eyes went wide as she jerked her head up to meet his gaze. "Are you serious?"

He shrugged. "It's no big deal. We have—no, I can't say that." His lips screwed up to one side. "My job is complex. I love it, but it requires a lot of me—of all of us. I'm happy to do it because I've seen the results."

Her lips screwed up on one side. "Okay, that sounds intense."

"It is. I'm not going to be home every night, and sometimes I travel. I have a house alarm that I don't use. The code is one eight six four three seven. I'll write it down, but you need to keep it somewhere secure. If you want to use it at night when I'm not here, that would be cool. I'll set your number up as the person to call if they need to validate an alarm is real. The password is volleyball if they call and you want them to disregard the alarm."

Audrey typed the information into her phone in a note. She met Tony's gaze, wondering again why he was being so nice to her. "Thank you for telling me about the alarm. That way, if I leave with Meredith, I'll feel safe coming back in."

His lips quirked up into a smile. "I want you to feel safe."

"I think I'm going to head to the school today. I'll get Meredith enrolled, then look for a job that is walking distance from here."

"We need to get you some form of transportation."

She nodded, then shook her head. "I have some money set aside, but I don't know how much I can spend without knowing what kind of job I can get."

"The future is scary. I get that. I know you are still processing. You did just escape from a terrible situation. Breathe. Get Meredith enrolled and take a few weeks to acclimate."

A heavy sigh escaped her lips. "I feel like I'm sponging off you."

"Don't." Tony checked the time and frowned. "I have to go. I'll text you later. It might be tomorrow morning or afternoon before I'm back here."

"Be safe and have a good day."

As Tony waved goodbye, her stomach twisted with desire she shouldn't be feeling. She poured herself a cup of coffee and stepped outside. The sun was just starting to lighten the horizon. She only wanted a few minutes of alone time, but the door opened behind her, and Meredith stepped out, rubbing her eyes.

"Hey, honey, how are you doing?"

"What time is it?"

"It's still early. Do you want to go back to sleep?"

"No."

"Have you used the bathroom?"

Her daughter rubbed her eyes more but said nothing, a sure sign she hadn't stopped in the bathroom. Audrey wished she had hours to drink in this view but being a mom meant being there.

"Let's go inside and take care of brushing your teeth and using the restroom, then we can eat breakfast."

"Can I watch TV?"

"Sure, love. After we do the bathroom and your teeth are taken care of."

Audrey made breakfast while Meredith stretched out on the couch, watching some cartoon. She'd made a mental note of the food the day before, and she wanted to head to a grocery store, but she wasn't sure how far away one was.

"Breakfast is done," Audrey said. Meredith didn't move. She was about to turn off the TV when her daughter got up and came to the table.

One of the many things she needed to do was fix her banking situation. She hadn't closed her bank account before leaving the States, and she didn't have access to that bank here. She'd have to figure out a solution. She still hadn't used her credit card because she feared it would pinpoint where she was. The banking side of her bank was paperless, but she feared if she used her credit card, they might send something to her parents' address which she'd used to set up her account. She should log on and change her mailing address, but again she worried the bank would send a notification of change of address. She should have thought about all of this and closed her account, withdrawing her money.

"Mommy, can we go to the park?"

"Sure, honey."

Audrey cleaned up their breakfast dishes before heading to her room to pull on some clothes. She'd washed their clothes yesterday and realized they didn't have enough shorts. She would have to take Meredith shopping at some point soon. Getting there would be the biggest struggle.

They headed to the park where Meredith played by herself until another family showed up with one little girl about Meredith's age and a boy around the same age.

"Hello," the woman who was probably their mother said as she stopped about ten feet away.

"Hi," Audrey said.

"Is your husband military?" the woman asked.

How could she explain her situation? No one would understand. Her husband wasn't military, he was a criminal, but no one needed that information.

"I'm visiting a friend." It was the truth, not the whole truth, but something close to the truth.

"Oh. How long will you be here?"

Audrey shrugged. "It's a long-term visit. I may stay for a while."

"We just moved here. My husband came over almost a month ago, and I moved here this week. I think I remember seeing you on the plane with your daughter."

Fear raced up Audrey's back so fast she stood. "Oh." Should she take off? Was this woman a plant from Eddy?

"I didn't mean to frighten you. I knew it would sound weird. I just...I'm sorry. I remember seeing you with a guy who looked military, and then he wasn't with you. It's none of my business. He just seemed like such a good father."

Audrey blew out a breath and shook her head. "No, he's just a friend."

"He was rather cute."

Audrey shouldn't be having this conversation. Her marriage to Eddy was over, but they were still married, and she wasn't free to date Tony. The fantasies she'd had about Tony had to stop. He wasn't interested in her like that.

"Just a friend, nothing more."

"So, will your daughter be in kindergarten?"

Audrey shook her head. "No, preschool. I was thinking about looking into the public program at the school down the street."

The woman's eyes narrowed. "Oh, so it is a long visit."

"I'll be here a few months, and I don't want her to get behind."

"Well, I guess we'll see you there. I just enrolled my two this morning."

Audrey nodded. She wasn't looking forward to the task but knew she needed to get it done. Before leaving Eddy, she'd been smart and had everything Meredith would need to start school. Now she just had to enroll her.

The woman checked her watch and cringed. "Shoot. I have to go. We have an appointment on the other side of Honolulu. It was nice chatting with you."

The woman took off, telling her kids to hustle. Meredith came over to Audrey with her lips down in a frown.

"Why'd they leave?"

"Their mother has an appointment. How about we walk over to the school and get you enrolled into the program?"

Meredith punched the air with her fist. "Yes! Brooke said she is going there."

"Is Brooke the little girl's name?"

"Yes. Her brother is Buster. That's an odd name."

Audrey nodded as she took Meredith's hand. "I'm sure it's a family name."

Meredith shrugged then skipped ahead on the sidewalk. If only Audrey felt so light and airy about their life. The weight of decisions that needed to be made had Audrey's stomach turning. They stopped by Tony's house to pick up her paperwork before heading to the school.

The enrollment meeting didn't take long, and luckily, Meredith was so young there wasn't an expectation of records to be sent. After they finished at the school, they walked back to Tony's house, and Audrey made them lunch.

Meredith fell asleep on the couch, giving Audrey time to think. She stepped outside and breathed in the fresh air. This place was heaven. She'd never been to Hawaii. The scenery wasn't tainted by Eddy, and she felt comfortable here. This was probably the last place Eddy would ever look for her.

A chill swept through her body. He would come after her if he ever found out where she was. She needed a job. Meredith would be enrolled in school. That gave her time. She didn't need much right now, just something to earn a little cash.

Fear slithered through her causing chills to spread over her shoulders and down her arms despite the warm weather. She drew in a breath, wondering if she was in the wrong. Had she made too many assumptions about Eddy?

The door opened behind her, and Meredith stood in the opening, rubbing her eyes. Audrey dropped to one of the chairs and held out her arms. Meredith moved quickly and settled on her lap, rubbing her eyes before closing them as she rested her head against Audrey's chest. She wasn't wrong for wanting to protect her child. She had no clue why someone like Tony had stepped in to help her, but she was thankful he had.

The evening with Meredith was like when they were on the mainland and on the run, but more relaxed. She didn't have to look over her shoulder, searching to find if someone had followed. She did set the alarm before leaving the house and walking to the park. Once there, she found the mother and two children she'd run into earlier.

"Hello," the woman called out.

Meredith waved then took off to play with Brooke. "I'm Audrey. I didn't get your name earlier."

"Liz. It's good to see you."

"Thank you. I got Meredith enrolled. She's in Mrs. Beazley's class."

"Wow, that's where Brooke will be."

"Well, then I guess it's good we met each other."

"It is. Davis is a year older than Brooke."

"Oh, Meredith thought his name was Buster."

Liz chuckled but rolled her eyes. "That's Chip's nickname for him. I hate it, but Chip is king where Bus—Davis is concerned."

Audrey stared out at the playground, wondering how many times she echoed the same thought. Eddy was king. Eddy's wants and needs superseded her own. Eddy was the man of the house, so she had to do what he wanted, be who he wanted, and never disobey him.

She didn't know this woman and couldn't tell her the truth about her previous life. For a brief moment, Audrey worried Eddy had sent Liz, but the woman wasn't hard enough to work for Eddy. She was nice to her children, and the kids seemed like regular kids.

Liz was just a regular woman who bowed to her husband's needs. Maybe Liz didn't have it that bad, but Audrey wouldn't dig. The last thing she needed was to take on someone else's problems. She had enough of her own.

CHAPTER 11

Tony stepped out of the building and headed to his SUV as the sun started its daily climb, turning the sky shades of pink and orange that looked more like a painting than real. Exhaustion filled him. They'd been up for most of the night, catching a few naps here and there. If he were on the mission, adrenaline would have kept him going. Sitting in a conference room at the base was safe and left him tired.

Few cars were on the freeway, and he made it home fast. Audrey hadn't called, and his alarm hadn't gone off. When he stepped into the house, everything was quiet. For a moment, he thought Audrey was still asleep, then he spied her outside on the grass, a towel beneath her as she bent low, and walked her hands away from her feet, keeping her butt up in the air before she moved slowly to the ground then lifted her chest, her back arched.

His stomach twisted, and his heart rate picked up. She moved smoothly, almost like her body flowed into the yoga positions. He imagined himself beside her, then under her as her round breasts grazed his pecs. A shiver rippled through him, leaving him feeling needy. He pushed away the thought of her moving against him, touching him, kissing him as he headed to the laundry room.

He dropped his dirty clothes in the washer and cringed. His stuff stank more than normal. He added extra soap so his clothes could soak once he started the wash. Maybe his clothes didn't stink more than usual, maybe he just didn't want Audrey to notice how gross he was.

Once in his room, he stripped then pulled on a pair of shorts so he could drop the clothes he'd worn into the washer along with all his other dirty clothes.

He was in the laundry room adding soap to the wash when the sound of the back door sliding closed hit him. He had to force himself to think pure thoughts of Audrey.

"Hello?" she called out from the kitchen.

He pushed open the laundry room door. "Hey, I

just got home. I'm going to shower, then drop into bed for a few hours."

"Oh." Audrey's eyes flicked over his chest, and her cheeks turned pink. She turned away from him and poured herself a mug of coffee. "I'll take Meredith to the park when she wakes up."

"That's not necessary. I'm tired. I'll sleep through almost anything."

Audrey turned to face him, her cheeks going pink again before she spun back to her coffee. "It's good for her to get out and run."

"Okay, it's up to you. We're having a picnic tomorrow morning with the crew. That way, you can meet everyone."

Worry filled her face. "I hope they don't think I'm taking advantage of you. I swear I'm moving toward getting a job. I just—"

He lifted his hand, stopping her words. "It's okay. No one will think you're taking advantage of me. It was my decision to invite you here."

She nodded but didn't look convinced. He thought about saying more, but he needed to get some rest. Sleep came easily, and he woke to sexy dreams of Audrey touching him. He blew out a breath and sat up, knowing he needed to take care of his dick in the shower but also that it would do little to get rid of the desire he felt for this off-limits woman.

He didn't want her to leave, but it was difficult having her here and not acting on his desires. He'd told her she would be safe in his house. Now he just needed to make sure she was safe, even from him.

On Saturday, he woke early and did a hard workout, ending with a six-mile run. As he approached the park near his house, he saw Audrey and Meredith. Normally he wouldn't stop to chat with anyone on his run, but he'd almost finished, and Meredith was waving at him from the play structure.

His chest seemed to expand as happiness filled him. That girl was special. He hoped he got the chance to see her grow up. Already she'd lodged herself into a special place in his heart.

"Hey, you look hot," Audrey said as he approached. Then she realized what she'd said, and her cheeks flamed red as the woman she was standing next to tried to hide her laughter.

Legs didn't want to embarrass Audrey more, so he didn't comment about what she'd said. Luckily for all of them, Meredith ran over.

"Why are you so wet?"

He smiled down at her. "I just ran six miles."

"I bet I could run six miles," Meredith said.

"I bet you could. We'll test that theory later. Right now, I'm going to get cleaned up, and then we get to go on a picnic at the beach."

"The beach!" Meredith yelled.

"We'll be there in a bit. That should give you time to shower."

"I'm in the Navy. I shower fast," Legs said.

"This is Liz. Her husband is in the Navy."

Liz stuck her hand out then pulled back as Legs lifted his hands. "Sorry, I'm a mess. I didn't know I'd see you all. Otherwise, I would have gone a different route and showered before coming over here."

"It's okay." Audrey's eyes narrowed. "Why is there dirt on your hands and chest?"

Legs looked at his hands and shrugged. "I did some burpees and other stuff on the run. I guess I got dirty."

Meredith ran back over after talking to her friends for a bit. "Are we going to the beach now?"

Legs chuckled. "I need to shower first. I'm taking off. So in about twenty minutes."

Meredith started clapping and jumping around as Legs headed out. He ran the last bit, kicking off his shoes on the patio before heading inside. He stank, his shoes probably smelled like death, and his pants were dripping. He wasn't used to having other people live with him. Usually, when he came home from a run, he stripped in his laundry room. He couldn't walk around the house naked, not with Meredith and Audrey living here. Some things would have to change.

The cold shower felt wonderful, and he dressed quickly, deciding his wet clothes needed to hang in the bathroom before taking them to the laundry room. He stepped out from his bedroom, tugging on his shirt, as the front door opened.

Audrey was talking to Meredith and didn't see him, which was fine by him. He liked watching her. Maybe he needed to find someone to blow off some steam with.

Hitting on Audrey would be wrong. She had enough trouble in her life. He'd invited her here with no strings attached, so he needed to stop trying to tie her down. She probably wasn't really interested in him. He might have a finely honed body with muscles for days, but that didn't mean she was attracted to him. Keeping Audrey and Meredith safe was his priority, not making a play for her.

CHAPTER 12

Apprehension chilled her to the bone. What if Tony's friends didn't like her? She wasn't trying to take advantage of a nice guy, but that's basically what she was doing. Tony had no clue she lusted after him.

She had no business lusting after anyone. Her marriage had been over for years, but she'd stayed. Now she knew that if she'd left, Eddy would have made her life miserable. He wasn't a good guy or even a halfway decent guy. He was a killer, a criminal, not at all what she'd thought he was when she'd married him.

She was still legally tied to Eddy, but she wanted nothing to do with him. Tony's friends would hate her if they knew. At least she would hate herself if she were in their position.

Tony pulled into the lot and turned to face her, his smile wide. "They're all here."

"Oh," was all she could muster.

"Mommy, look, the beach." Meredith was bouncing in her seat, ready to run to the sand and play.

Audrey wished she had half of Meredith's enthusiasm. She was excited, but the fear had grown. What if they didn't like her at all? She'd been bullied at one point in high school. What if these women were like that? It could easily go wrong.

Tony got Meredith out of the back while she stepped out from the passenger side. Everything seemed to go slower than normal. It was almost like she was detached from everything. Maybe it was distraction or just an overall feeling of disconnection from what should be happening and what was happening.

"Legs," one of the guys called out as he came over, grabbing the bag of food Tony had brought. "And this must be Meredith. Our kids are much younger than you. But I bet they'd love to watch you play."

"Hi!" Meredith bounced on her feet as she waved with both hands.

The two-hand wave thing was different. Maybe Meredith was just excited and possibly a little nervous. Audrey had noticed that her own attitude influenced Meredith. But her daughter didn't seem to have any problem meeting new people as she took off running to the group with the two babies and way too many people for Audrey to remember their names.

The man who'd introduced himself to Meredith came around the SUV and stuck out his hand. "I'm Vine. My real name is Jason. You can call me either. Everyone is excited to meet you."

"God, I'm sweating bullets." She hadn't meant to say that out loud. The cringe was automatic, but both Tony and Jason laughed it off.

"We won't bite. The women don't know exactly why you're over here in Hawaii, so it's up to you how much you tell them, but Legs ran the whole thing down with me."

She turned to Tony, her eyes wide. "So he knows and doesn't hate me?"

Jason threw back his head, laughing hard. "No way I would hate you. Come on and meet the gang."

Audrey felt like it was the first day in a new school. Embarrassment filled her. What if she said or did something wrong?

Jason introduced her to the group, going down the list of couples who paired up so she could see who went with who. There was Jason and Jenna, Ethan and Sunshine, Robert and Ashley, and Jordan, who went by Quirk.

"The other guy on our team just left, and we don't have another regular yet," Tony said.

Jason shrugged. "You would have liked Becky and Forest. The new guy should be here next week…maybe."

"You already know who he is?" one of the guys asked as they moved away, following Meredith to the water.

Audrey wondered if she should go down with them when Sunshine came over, a wide smile on her face. "You'll figure out their names soon. I had to write them all down in my phone."

"Oh my goodness," Jenna laughed as she stepped close, a baby in her arms. "They're good guys. This is Lila."

"And this chunk is Oliver," the other woman said.

"This is embarrassing. I don't remember your name," Audrey said.

"Ashley. And don't worry about it. We should wear name tags for the first few times meeting you, but the guys nixed that idea."

"They're great guys, but they would rather talk to you than display their name," Sunshine said.

"So, how long have you been in Hawaii?" Ashley asked.

Audrey tried not to cringe as fear wove through her. She didn't want to answer too many questions and reveal the truth about her past. "A few days."

Jenna lifted her eyebrows. "Do you like it?"

"I've been at home with Meredith for the most part." They all turned to watch Meredith laugh and tumble with a couple of the guys. "They're good with kids."

"They are all very responsible men. Their jobs are tough, but they are still kids at heart. They play like they're in junior high. I bet they'd play chase for hours with her," Jenna said.

Audrey liked how the guys were keeping Meredith busy. She probably was bored having to hang out all day with her. Hopefully, the school would be good, and she'd make a few friends.

Sunshine moved to the grill and flipped the burgers. Jenna and Ashley set their babies in playpens they had set up under the shade. Some of the guys came over, and Meredith wanted some water.

Then the food was done, and they all sat down to eat. Audrey felt a little odd listening to their conversations about work, their week, people they all knew, but she didn't. She wasn't dating Tony, but none of them joked with him about relationships or women, though they did say something to Jordan about a woman he had gone out with.

After they ate, the guys went for a walk with Meredith. Tony promised they would keep her safe, and Audrey decided to hang back with the women. She's spent so much time with Meredith, and she knew her daughter needed a break.

The women all laughed at something. Audrey hadn't been paying close enough attention to know what they were talking about. She turned, trying to figure out what they'd said.

"You know how it is. Right?" Ashley asked.

"I'm sorry, I was…sorry. My mind is elsewhere." Audrey felt bad about not listening.

"Jenna was saying that even when they're tired, they still want to get busy. You probably haven't been with Tony long enough to—"

She shook her head, not wanting a lie to come between them later. "Oh, we're not together."

The women all blinked at her, and Jenna narrowed her gaze. "Why? I mean, I love Vine, but Tony is hot."

Audrey's cheeks heated. Jenna was right. Tony was very hot, but she couldn't. She blew out a breath and shook her head. "He's just being nice. He's not interested in me."

"The way he was looking at you early begs to differ," Ashley said.

Audrey shook her head. "No, he really is just being nice. I was in a bad spot, and he helped."

Jenna moved closer and took her hand. "What happened?"

Heat washed over Audrey. These women wouldn't understand what she'd gone through. Heck, she didn't understand it sometimes. She should have left, but she hadn't. Eddy was a killer, and she was still married to him. She needed to get a divorce. But how could she do that and not inform him where she was? She was screwed.

"It's hard to explain." Audrey shrugged, not wanting to divulge too much and get judged for how stupid she'd been.

"We understand hard to explain things," Jenna said as she picked up her fussy baby and held him close. "We've all experienced some trouble."

"I was held hostage by a prostitution ring in Indonesia," Ashley said.

"My brother kidnapped me and held me in chains in his house. Jenna and Ashley are great. They haven't ever held it against me. When they found out what had happened, I was worried they would never want to speak to me again, but they were wonderful. Robert has been awesome. He's stood by me through it all. I've had to unload a lot of stuff in therapy, but these people are great. My past hasn't made them hate me."

Sunshine's words brought tears to Audrey's eyes. Could she trust them? Embarrassment flooded her. She was about to say something when the guys came running back with Meredith.

"Mommy, you have to see this. We found a dolphin. Hurry."

"Sorry, I need—"

"Go. We're fine," Jenna said.

Audrey felt relieved she didn't have to tell these women what had gone wrong in her life. She hated that she'd stayed married to Eddy. She didn't regret having Meredith, but every other part of her relationship with Eddy brought up one misgiving after another. She wanted her life to be easier, but right now, she'd have to settle for this.

CHAPTER 13

He loved and hated having Audrey live with him. He needed a real release so he'd gone to a bar two weeks after Audrey had moved in, thinking that finding some woman for a one-night stand would alleviate his issues. He couldn't do it. He couldn't get past the idea that the woman wasn't Audrey. He knew if he screwed someone else, he'd feel like he was cheating. Never, in all of his years of dating, had he ever cheated and though Audrey wasn't his, he felt like there was something between them.

Having Meredith in his house had been a blast. He enjoyed hearing about her day. She was funny and engaging in a way he didn't think kids could be. He couldn't imagine life without her, and he couldn't imagine his life without Audrey.

Some days, after Meredith was in bed, he and Audrey would sit on the back patio watching the stars and talking about life. Many of those nights, he thought about what would happen if he leaned over and kissed her. He hadn't touched her yet, but he wanted to. Her life was full of complications, but that didn't stop his desire.

Audrey found a job working during the hours Meredith was in school. The job was close by, so she rode a bike she'd found abandoned behind a grocery store. It needed new tires, which he'd bought, but otherwise, the bike was fine and hadn't cost Audrey anything.

He had an odd day off because they had worked all night long again while another team ran a mission. He woke at one and found Audrey at home. She'd just come out of the shower and was standing in the hall in a towel that barely covered her ass. When he opened his door, she spun around, gasping and trying to cover herself.

"Oh God, I didn't realize you were back," Audrey said.

Desire shot straight to his dick. He tried to keep his eyes up, but he drank her in like a fine wine. He wanted to touch her creamy skin as he pulled her close, kissing down the long column of her neck to her shoulders then lower, to the mounds barely contained by the towel.

Legs cleared his throat as he dragged his eyes up to meet hers. "I should have texted you that I was home." Heat filled him as his cock grew hard.

"No, it's—I'm sorry. I shouldn't be..." Audrey looked down, her cheeks turning an even darker red as she moved quickly to her room.

After about twenty minutes, Audrey came out of her room. She wasn't able to meet his gaze. He needed her to get past this so they could move on.

"Listen, it's okay. We're bound to run into each other in the halls."

"I shouldn't be here." Audrey made a sound like a sob.

Legs didn't even think twice about moving to Audrey and pulling her into a hug. Her body shook as she cried. The tears fell for a good five minutes, and he tried hard not to feel any desire, but having her close was messing with his mind.

She wiped her face and glanced up without stepping back. He saw it then, the desire he had for her shining back at him. A shiver skated his nerves. Could she want him, too?

Legs felt like his mouth had dried out, and his body craved water, but only Audrey had the water.

He needed to feel her lips on his and drink from her magnificence.

They both adjusted a little, leaving them only inches apart. He licked his lips, wishing there was an easy way for them to be together.

Audrey drew in a shuddering breath and stepped back. "I can't pull you deeper into my crap. I'm sorry. I can pack a bag—"

A hole opened in his chest and he reached out and grabbed her arm. "Don't."

Her gaze met his, and she paused. "I haven't even filed for divorce."

Legs groaned, then reached up and raked his fingers through his hair. Desire pumped hard, and he knew she would be safer from desire if she left, but that would make her too big of a target. She would have to be sloppy, make amends, and possibly reveal herself and her location to Eddy. "I can't lie and say I'm not attracted to you."

Her breath hitched. "Should I move out?"

He shook his head. "No. We can be adults about this."

"That's what I fear."

He met her gaze and saw laughter in her eyes. "I won't touch you."

She swallowed hard, lust replacing the laughter.

"I have almost two thousand dollars saved up. I want to talk to a lawyer." Her eyes flicked to his lips for just a second and he understood loud and clear what she wanted.

"Make an appointment, and I can go with you."

Audrey shook her head. "That might make it confusing. I need this to be as uncomplicated as possible."

"You're going to have to tell the lawyer what you saw. He needs to know to protect himself and his family."

Audrey gasped. "I hadn't even thought about that."

"Once you file, you'll have to be prepared for anything. This house is owned by my aunt who has a different last name. I'm renting, but my name isn't on the mortgage or tied to the property. That doesn't mean he won't come looking. Maybe he's found out my name from the hotel in California, or maybe not."

Audrey closed her eyes and blew out a breath. Legs pulled her close again. At first, she resisted, then rested her head against his chest. It felt right holding her. He closed his eyes and imagined this was their life, not the pain and fear but the comfort of having Audrey in his arms.

"We'll figure this out," Legs said.

"Why are you being so nice to me?" Audrey asked.

"Because you don't deserve the shit Eddy put you through. You deserve to have a good life."

"Are you sure? I feel like I'm not a good person. I saw someone get murdered, and I was too afraid to say anything. I should have gone to the cops."

He cupped her face, forcing himself to keep his distance and not lean in to kiss her. He wanted to so badly, but she needed to feel safe. "You did what you thought you had to do to survive. If you'd gone to the cops, you wouldn't be here now, and you know it."

She blinked up at him with wide eyes. "I'm scared."

"I'm sure you are. I'm here for you."

Audrey shivered. "You are very good-looking."

Her words brought a smile to his face. "Thank you, and I find you very attractive." He took a step back. "But we're going to be good. Not because I'm not interested, but I can tell you need your life with Eddy to be over. You'll move your divorce along, and we'll see how things go."

Audrey's eyebrows pinched together, and she

rolled her lips in before shaking her head. "I need to go get Meredith from the bus stop."

"I'll go with you," Legs said.

"Are you sure?"

"Yes. I want to spend more time with you."

She blew out a breath. "It's weird being here in Hawaii."

"How so?" Legs asked.

"Eddy has no clue where I am. I feel safe. I hate that we're still married. I want to be free from him. I fear that as soon as I file, he'll try to get full custody of Meredith."

"He might try, but you have the law on your side. You saw Eddy murder someone. The judge will take that into account."

"I hope it's that easy. I don't know what Eddy will do once I file. If he figures out where I am, it will be all over."

"We just have to keep him away from you."

They walked up to the corner, waving at the other women who were picking up their kids. It was a little uncomfortable since one of the moms flirted heavily with him. He wanted to tell her to back off, but he didn't want to make a scene and embarrass Audrey.

Once Meredith came running off the bus, they

each took one of her hands and headed back to his place. This felt right. His heart filled with an emotion he'd never felt before. He wanted more of this.

Meredith kept them entertained for a few hours. She seemed exhausted but didn't want to go to sleep. Eventually, she got into bed close to eight. When Audrey stepped out from Meredith's room, Legs had to swallow down the desire pumping through him. He wanted to have her in his arms, but not yet. They had time.

The attraction he felt for Audrey wasn't going away. He found her interesting, and he just hoped that when the time came for her to be free, she felt the same about him.

CHAPTER 14

The eggshells she and Tony had been walking on seemed broken under their shoes. They both knew they were attracted to each other, but she was still bound by a vow she'd made years ago to a man she didn't really know. Why had she agreed to marry Eddy?

Young and stupid, she'd followed what her parents had suggested. They'd told her Eddy was her best bet. He had money, but she had no self-respect. She'd sold her soul to the devil to be with Eddy, or at least that's how she felt. Now she wanted her soul to be her own, but she couldn't find a way to free herself of Eddy without endangering Meredith.

Tony was working late again. It didn't happen

often, but there were some days he had to stay. The military was fair with him, though he told her sometimes he had to leave for weeks on end, and he would have no idea when he would be home.

It was lonely when he wasn't home, but she listened to music to keep bad thoughts from running her to the ground. Today, worry ate at her as she stepped outside and blinked against the bright sun. The brightness felt like a betrayal, trying to shine the light on everything wrong in her life. Or maybe she was the betrayal. Flying to Hawaii with Tony, ripping Meredith away from everything she knew, taking her to a new place to start school though she had a home in New York. Was she totally mental? What kind of mother did that to her child?

Eddy couldn't really have been that bad. Could he have? Audrey closed her eyes, thinking about the body, the drugs, and everything else she'd seen. Maybe she misunderstood Eddy. Had she really seen what she thought she had? The bags of drugs under Meredith's bed had been the last straw. She hadn't really been surprised when he'd come home smelling like other women. She'd tried to come up with a good explanation for his actions. Even when she'd been deep in denial, thinking it all had been staged, she couldn't let go of the questions of why Eddy would allow her to think he'd killed someone. None of her excuses for him made sense.

They'd lost touch with each other, and she'd about lost her mind. They hadn't even slept in the same room for the last two years. Her marriage had been over for a long time. The only good thing she'd gotten out of the deal had been Meredith. Now she needed to file for a divorce, but she knew doing that would put her and her daughter in danger.

Eddy would switch it around, blame her for all the bad in their marriage. She had no proof he'd killed anyone, she didn't have the drugs, she had no records of his misdeeds, just rotten memories that wouldn't stand up against him in court.

If he tried to take Meredith back, she would be screwed. Judges liked giving fifty-fifty split custody now. No way she could stay in Hawaii. If she lived close to Eddy, he would know where she was. He may not kill her, but he would make her life miserable. He wasn't above petty deeds to make her unhappy.

She had a choice, stay here in Hawaii and live a simple life, never connecting with Tony, or file for divorce, and pray Eddy didn't try to kill her. Either way, she was sure her life was screwed.

Meredith's bus would be dropping her off soon,

and she needed to head out to get her. Her phone rang, and she picked it up, thinking nothing of answering.

"You thought you could hide."

The voice slid through her like ice, leaving behind huge goosebumps. She hung up and turned off her phone. Maybe he didn't know where she was. How could he have gotten her number? She'd been careful. She had a burner phone, and few people had the number. Her work, friends, and Meredith's school had the number.

"Oh shit, Meredith."

She took off running up the road, praying the bus was on time. She needed to find her daughter. If Eddy had Meredith, she would die. She couldn't let him get her. He held no affection toward Meredith, and he probably wouldn't think twice about disposing of her. She wasn't important, or she hadn't ever been important to him in the past. The only thing he would find important about Meredith was using her as a tool to manipulate Audrey.

She would jump through any hoop to save her daughter, and Eddy knew that now. When Meredith had first been born, Eddy had no clue how important she was to Audrey. He'd only seen their daughter as an inconvenience. After the murder she'd witnessed, he'd learned that threatening Meredith got her to do what he wanted.

She was out of breath, so she slowed, trying to look as normal as possible as her gaze swept over the parents waiting for their children. No one looked weird or out of place. It was the usual crowd of parents and caregivers waiting for their charges.

The bus's wheels squeaked and complained as the large vehicle slowed beside them. Audrey held her breath while the first few kids got off. Then three more came hopping down the bus stairs. She'd counted the kids before and knew ten children got off at this stop. That meant there would be three more children. She prayed Meredith was in the group.

One child stumbled off looking like the world had stepped on him and ground him in the dirt. Then another child bounded off, flinging herself in her mother's arms. Audrey's chest tightened, and her head spun. Where was Meredith?

Then she saw another child, and her breath rushed out as she dropped to her knees and pulled Meredith into a hug. It may have been overly dramatic, but she'd been so worried, and now she knew Eddy didn't have Meredith.

"Stop squeezing so hard," Meredith complained

as she tried to push her way out of her mother's arms.

Audrey stood and patted Meredith on the head. "Sorry. I got a little carried away."

"I want ice cream."

"Let's go home. I think we have some in the refrigerator."

"Yea!" Meredith cheered as she took off toward Tony's house.

Audrey couldn't help but look back, trying to figure out if Eddy had someone stalking them. She didn't see anyone waiting, but she didn't trust Eddy. How had he gotten her phone number?

Once she got home, she turned on the alarm but bypassed the sliding glass door to the backyard and grabbed two bowls for ice cream. Her day had been bad, and she needed something to help calm her down. Ice cream was better than a beer, or at least she thought it was since Tony wouldn't be home until later.

Somehow, she lasted until Meredith's bedtime without losing her mind. By the time she stepped out of Meredith's room, she was beside herself. She hadn't turned her phone back on, and she wondered if Tony had called.

Before giving Meredith her bath, she'd turned the alarm off then reset it with all the doors and windows armed. Fear was winning this battle, but she still had a sliver of belief that Eddy wasn't in Hawaii. Tony had promised her someone was watching Eddy's information, making sure he didn't travel. An alert would have been sent if he'd bought an airline ticket. But what if Eddy hired someone new? What if he sent them to search out her location?

She sat at the kitchen table and pushed the button to turn on her phone. Her hands shook as she stared at the screen, praying Eddy hadn't called. Her phone turned on, and the blips and pings started to show up. Audrey drew in a slow breath, the pressure of being found out creating a dull ache in the back of her skull that grew and circled her head.

The texts were easiest to look at, and she stared at the words as they blurred from her tears. Eddy threatened to find her and beat her, said he would hang her from a tree, or maybe he would let his friends take turns before he beat her to death.

Tears streamed down her cheeks. Eddy hated her. He promised to get back at her for leaving. The door opened, and she might have let out a yelp.

"Hey, Audrey, I was—what's wrong?" Tony asked as he punched in the code to turn off the alarm.

She didn't know what to do. The urge to hide the texts blossomed inside, but Tony couldn't help her if he didn't know what he was up against. She held out her phone and let him get a look.

His jaw tightened, making him look angrier than she'd ever seen him. His nostrils flared, and his lips thinned.

"I don't know what to do," Audrey whispered.

"I'm sending everything to a friend. He's good at analyzing stuff. I'm calling in a favor, too. Just give me a moment."

"Tony," Audrey said.

He paused and blinked at her, going from looking scary to sitting in the chair beside her, trying to look like the man she'd started to fall for.

"Hey, we're going to keep you safe. I have people who are excellent at this kind of stuff. I also have a friend who is a decent guy, but he would have no problem taking Eddy off the planet."

"Is he like Eddy, you know, killing people?"

"If he's killed someone, it's because they were abusing women, children, or animals. He wouldn't kill someone over money. He's a fair man, but he's not into sugar coating anything. Let me send these to my friends, and then we'll piece through everything."

"I can't let him have Meredith back."

Tony cupped her cheek and leaned in, not kissing her. Instead, he rested his forehead against hers, breathing slowly. His slow breaths and gentle touch centered her. The wild, uncontrollable feelings eased as she tried to match her breath to his.

"He's never getting Meredith back. I won't allow it."

Audrey knew he meant those words. She heated food for him while he worked to download all the voicemails. She hadn't listened to any of them, and she worried what Eddy had said. Would these men look down on her and Meredith because Eddy was such a jerk?

After Tony finished eating, a knock sounded at the door, and her head whipped up. She met Tony's gaze, but he held up his hand, reassuring her everything was fine.

"That should be the guy helping us." Tony checked the peephole before opening the door.

"You have a problem?" the man asked in a gruff voice.

"Come in. This is Audrey. Her daughter, Meredith, is asleep."

"I'm Rawlins." He didn't try to shake her hand. Instead, he stood off to the side, his lips down in a frown. He looked like he'd seen some shit and could probably take on the world.

"I've sent you the texts, and I'm downloading the voicemails," Tony said.

"First off, he thinks you're in California," Rawlins said.

Audrey narrowed her gaze. "California? Why does he think that?"

"The area code. I skimmed the texts after I printed them out. There's one stating he was flying to California to track you down. He still doesn't know where you are. How did he find the phone number?"

Audrey shook her head. "I don't know."

"The only people who have the number are people we trust and the school," Tony said.

"Oh shit." Audrey whipped her head up, meeting Tony's gaze. She'd screwed up, and her mess up made her want to toss her cookies.

"What?" Rawlins asked.

"Music. When I signed up for a music service, I had to give my phone number. I put my old address with Eddy, so I thought I was safe. But I had to add my phone number. I used an old email address, and I guess he figured it out." Tears streamed down her cheeks. She hid her face as embarrassment slid through her. "I'm so sorry."

Tony stepped close and pulled her to him. She rested her head against his shoulder, wishing Eddy would go away. "It's okay. It could have been much worse. We need to get you a new online identity."

"Still no photos, though," Rawlins said.

She nodded as she stepped away from Tony, wiping her eyes on a napkin before blowing her nose. "I'm stupid for signing up for that music. I made you drive all the way over here."

"It's fine," Rawlins said. "I needed to be in the area for another matter. And if you see me around, don't act like you know me. Nothing against you, but if I'm surveilling the surrounding area, I don't want to alert anyone that I'm around. I'm not saying Eddy or his people are here, but this was a good test run to see how we can respond. People make mistakes, and now you know to change all of your email addresses."

"I was using Tony's email for Meredith's school. I'm not on social media. I just wanted to listen to some music and didn't think to use Tony's email address."

Rawlins's lips thinned. "You need to keep an eye out. Legs told me you were looking into seeing a lawyer. I'm going to get transcripts made of those voicemails. Don't get rid of that phone, but you need to get a new one. When you see the lawyer, I'd like to go with you. I want the lawyer to understand just how deranged Eddy is."

Audrey bit her lower lip and nodded. More tears trickled down her cheeks. "I can't believe you all are so nice to me."

Rawlins's lips twitched up in what might have been a smile. "I've spent my life defending those who couldn't stand up for themselves. It's what I do."

"Thank you."

"I don't do it for thanks. I do it because it's the right thing to do. Stay safe and keep your daughter safe. I know you're doing all you can. Keep at it. Eventually, you'll be free from that clown and have a life you want."

Tony walked Rawlins out, then came back in and set the alarm. Audrey moved to Tony, wrapping her arms around his waist as he pulled her close. His lips brushed over her forehead, and a shiver rippled through her. She wanted more with this man, but she didn't feel like she could act on her desires. It wouldn't be fair to Tony to get involved now.

Maybe one day she would be free to have something more than friendship with Tony, but for now, she would have to accept that a relationship with Tony would have to wait. Hopefully, he understood.

CHAPTER 15

Legs didn't yell at Audrey though the fear he'd felt mixed with the anger at her creating an account that could be traced to her left him feeling agitated. She'd messed up. But everyone messed up at some point, and there was no need to be a jerk. She felt terrible, and she'd learned a lesson.

Audrey sniffed as she stepped away from him. She picked up his dishes and loaded the dishwasher before setting it to run. She turned to stare at him. He stopped and glanced up to meet her gaze. Her forehead had deep wrinkles, and her eyes were sad. He didn't want her to be so upset. Her mistake was fixable.

"I'm really sorry."

The anguish in her voice made his stomach

clench. He wanted to go to her and pull her into a hug, but they weren't a couple. He couldn't force her to break a vow, even if that vow was with a piece of shit guy who didn't deserve her. "It's okay. You learned never to use that old email address."

She nodded, looking a little distant. "I'll pick up a new phone when I get to work. I'll text you the phone number."

He smiled, hoping she could pull herself out of the emotional hole she'd dug. "We'll work on getting you a new email address and accounts with fresh passwords he won't be able to guess."

Her breath hitched, and he couldn't stop himself. He moved to her, holding her close. She had made a critical error that reminded her how cruel Eddy was. He hadn't read all the texts, but he'd read enough to piss him off. The man was an asshole. He didn't respect Audrey at all, and there was no way he loved his daughter based on what he said he would do to her. They weren't safe with Eddy out in the world, and no matter how much Audrey wanted to protect Meredith, the girl was at risk. Eddy couldn't be trusted, but taking him out without provocation would be just as bad as what Eddy had done. They needed a way to get the cops to arrest him.

Legs needed to think on the matter. Maybe with

Rawlins, Tex, and the rest of the guys helping, he could somehow keep Audrey and Meredith safe.

The next few days were busy with his work, and then Meredith came down with something that shot her fever up over one hundred. They ended up taking her to a clinic on Saturday and getting a prescription for an ear infection.

Finally, about a week after the initial scare from Eddy, he and Audrey sat down and created a new email address they confirmed through Legs' account. Audrey knew she had to be extra careful now.

"The phone Eddy texted, should I keep it off or turn it on every few days?" Audrey asked.

"Why don't you let me have that. Then you don't have to listen to or read the crap he sends."

Pain flashed across Audrey's face. The more pain she suffered, the harder Legs found it to ignore his desire. She needed comfort, and he wanted to help. Sliding up to her and wrapping his arm around her shoulders, pulling her close, wouldn't do any harm, or would it? She'd held back multiple times. He'd seen the desire in her eyes, and then she'd shuttered the desire, leaving a blank look on her face. He had to respect her decision to not get involved.

"That would be best." Audrey stood, her eyes

averted from his. "I'm going to bed."

"Sure."

Legs got up and headed to the kitchen to make sure coffee was set up in the morning. A noise sounded behind him, and he turned to find Audrey standing in the doorway, her gaze on him, desire evident as the moon in the sky on a clear summer's night.

Neither of them moved or looked away. Legs' chest tightened as lust pumped through him. He needed to get this under control.

"I'm sorry," Audrey whispered.

"For what?" Legs couldn't imagine what she had to be sorry for. She hadn't done anything wrong.

"This is too hard on you. I shouldn't be here."

He took a step closer and stopped, knowing if he touched her, their desire would explode. "We've managed so far."

She nodded. "It's just getting harder. You're so nice. I should look for a place to live."

"You don't have enough money."

"No, but I can't put you in this situation. It's unfair."

This time he moved close but didn't touch her. If eyes could caress, hers certainly had, and he hoped he showed the same caring toward her. He wanted her to know if they were free, he would be loving, not harsh.

"You aren't putting me in any situation I'm not willingly staying in. If I wanted you out, you wouldn't be here. I don't mind if it takes a while for you to end your marriage."

Her lips pressed together, and her nose wrinkled. "God, I hate that I'm still married to him. I didn't even try to divorce before I ran."

"You ran because you weren't safe."

Audrey's gaze flicked to his lips. "If I were free, I wouldn't be sleeping in a different bed than you."

His chest tightened even more as his balls pulled up. "If you were free, I would have asked you to sleep with me much earlier."

Audrey's lips twisted as she tilted her head to the side. "Maybe this is better?"

Legs groaned as his dick jerked. "How is this better?"

"We have time to get to know one another. We get to view the bad habits without the rose tinting of sex hazing everything we look at."

He nodded. "When I work out, I stink. I know that much."

Her gaze flitted from his face to his chest, and a shiver shook her. "But the results are worth it."

Heat rushed to his face. "Are you ogling my muscles?"

Her cheeks turned pink. "Sorry."

"Don't apologize. I don't mind."

She cleared her throat and took a step back. "When we're free to do more, I hope you're not disappointed."

He shook his head. "Why would I be?"

"I'm not experienced. I don't know much other than what...well, I've only ever been with one person."

He reached out and cupped her cheek. "I don't care how experienced you are. Learning each other is so much more important than what you've done in the past."

Her breath hitched, and he dropped his hand. "Go on to bed. I'll make sure everything is locked up. We'll figure this out. In the meantime, let's have some fun together and enjoy each other's company."

She nodded and stepped back before turning and heading to her bedroom. When she closed the door, Legs gripped the counter, knowing tonight he'd hit the shower again and jack off to thoughts of Audrey. He didn't know if he could stand waiting, but he would have to because there was no way he would force her to do something she wasn't ready for.

CHAPTER 16

Doing Thanksgiving in Hawaii was interesting. Tony's team had the holiday weekend off, and they all got together to celebrate at a park. They still didn't have a full-time sixth person on their team, so it was just the five guys, Sunshine, Ashley, and Jenna.

There were loads of people enjoying the beach, spending the holiday with family, and having a good time. It was warm, which was a huge difference from Thanksgiving in New York. Meredith had fun playing with the guys and then entertaining the babies by doing somersaults and attempting cartwheels. Quirk came over and helped her get the cartwheel correct.

"Wow, Quirk," Jenna called out. "I didn't know you could do that."

Quirk laughed as his huge smile spread. "I was on my junior high cheerleading team, along with football."

"How did that work out?" Tony asked.

"I only cheered during basketball season. It's just something I did. I was good at it, too."

"So why didn't you cheer in high school?" Audrey asked.

Quirk shrugged. "I thought about it, but the bullying was taking its toll. I gave it up to prove I was something. Found out in the military that didn't matter. I should have stuck with gymnastics. That would have made it easier to pass BUDs."

Audrey squinched up her nose as confusion worked through her. "BUDs. What's that?"

"You haven't told her?" Ashley turned to Tony, her eyes wide.

Tony shrugged. "What? We haven't talked about that."

The food was ready, and they grabbed plates, but Tony's answer bugged her. They hadn't talked about a lot of stuff, and the reason was her fault. She'd brought too much stress with her, and they couldn't even have a real relationship.

Though she had a good time with Tony and his

friends, the conversation about BUDs bugged her. She said nothing, and tried to forget about it, but even days later she wanted to know.

Really, she wanted to know everything about Tony, but they weren't at that point in their relationship. They were friends and did things together like cook dinner when he was home, and spend time with Meredith at the park, but she wanted to curl up next to him at night and learn about his life.

Tony's work got busier since the new guy finally showed up the week after Thanksgiving. His name was Daniel, but they called him Dunk. She didn't understand the nickname thing, but then again, they didn't talk much about the Navy.

Eventually, she would talk to Tony about his life, but it seemed like too much conspired against them. Every time she thought they would have time for a conversation, something came up.

The week before Christmas, Meredith's school had a party, and Audrey took the day off work to attend. The school had gone all out and set up carnival games for the kids. Everyone was having fun.

Audrey relaxed enough to enjoy herself. This was

her first Christmas in a long time without the pressures Eddy put on her. Tony said he just wanted a simple day. She'd bought Meredith a few inexpensive items for under the tree, and she'd found something she thought Tony would appreciate.

Liz introduced Audrey to two of the women sitting close to her. "This is Cindy and Elle."

"Hi, it's nice to meet you." Audrey hadn't made friends with other women in the neighborhood. Maybe she should make more of an effort but with work and Meredith, she didn't have time.

"We're doing drinks a few days after Christmas. You should come," Liz said.

"I need to check with Tony." Audrey wasn't sure she wanted to do drinks with Liz. Maybe that was just the insecurity talking. She should go out, but who would watch Meredith?

"No. Don't let him stop you," Cindy said.

"You can bring Meredith over, and my sitter will watch them," Liz said.

Audrey didn't want to take advantage of anyone, and she felt like this was cutting it close. "Are you sure?"

Liz laughed as she nodded. "I'm positive. We'll have a blast."

"Let's take a photo," Cindy said.

"I'll take it," Audrey offered.

Liz reached for her, pulling her close. "Oh no, you have to be in it."

Audrey backed away and held out her hand for the phone. "I'm fine taking it. Besides, you all have known each other longer."

After taking the picture, Meredith came over and asked Audrey to push her on the swing. Happy for the excuse to leave and avoid conflict about the photo not including her, she followed Meredith to the playground and spent the next hour with her daughter, laughing and having a great time.

They headed home close to three, both of them exhausted. She still needed to buy a car, but the school wasn't too far from Tony's house, so she'd put off the purchase as she saved money.

Her job wasn't great, but they hadn't complained when she asked off for the full school break. Now she wouldn't have to hire a sitter.

She'd thought about begging off for the drinks with Liz and her friends. Her secrets were numerous, and she didn't want to tell everyone why she couldn't be in pictures that would be loaded onto social media. Not everyone was as accepting as Tony.

At least she had Tony she could depend on, even if she didn't have other friends. Before leaving Eddy, she'd lived a lonely existence. Why should she expect anything different now?

CHAPTER 17

Legs fired off two rounds then rolled to his right, scrambling up behind the rock before running to the next location where he would fire off another two rounds. They were working on accuracy when on the move. It would be great if every shot they took could be done with preparations, measurements, and time, but when being fired upon, they didn't always have time to think, much less measure wind speed. He'd hit the target eight times and fired ten. That wasn't too bad, but he needed to improve.

"Damn, Legs, that wasn't bad," Dunk said.

Legs chuckled. He didn't know Dunk well enough to know if he liked him or not, but so far, they were all getting along. Dunk was young. He'd joined the Navy to become a SEAL. Said he'd been training for years before he was old enough to join up.

"What was your score?" Legs asked.

"I only got six out of ten. I need to work on my shooting," Dunk said.

Legs nodded as they watched Vine run the course. He hit the target nine times out of the ten.

"I'm impressed," Dunk said about Vine.

Legs laughed. "Vine is a miracle worker on this course."

"You calling me a miracle?" Vine asked.

"Sure," Legs said.

"I'll give you a miracle," Vine said as he cupped his crotch.

They all laughed, even the men running the course. He liked that Dunk fit their humor and hadn't complained about the jokes they told. He missed Astro, but Dunk wasn't half bad. Dunk also wasn't an officer, so it would be a long time before they lost anyone else to promotion since none of them were jockeying to lead a team.

"So you still haven't slept with her?" Minx asked.

"Nope," Legs said as he began the task of breaking down his rifle.

"I don't get it," Dunk said. "She's living with you, but you aren't sleeping with her."

Legs shook his head. "She's not ready."

"How long does it take you to get a girl ready?" Dunk asked. "I mean, at most, it takes me an hour, and then they're squealing to get into my pants."

Legs rolled his eyes. "She isn't a girl, she's a lady, and I'm not trying to fuck her. I want her for more."

"Wow. What more are you expecting from her?" Dunk asked.

Vine burst out laughing. "One day, you'll tire of the fuck bunnies and want a woman you want to spend time with."

"Doubt it," Dunk said. "I have no use for a woman after I get off. I don't want anyone there in the morning or later in the day when I'm trying to watch a game or play something on the PlayStation."

Minx dropped a few napkins next to Dunk and walked off. Dunk grabbed them and shook them at Minx.

"What's this for?"

"For your date with yourself later since you don't need women."

Dunk wadded up the paper towels. "Hey, I can get any woman I want. I just don't want them." He tossed the wad toward the trash and missed.

"Why is your nickname Dunk if you miss that wide-ass trash can?" Wig asked.

Dunk got up, picked up the paper, and tossed it into the trash. "You all will find out, anyway. I can't do the toss trash into a basket thing. It just doesn't work. I have to dunk it in, or I miss."

"So is that why you don't want to date the same woman long-term?" Wig asked.

Dunk shook his head. "What?"

"Cause you keep missing the hole." Wig moved like he had his arms and one leg wrapped around someone. When he spoke, he pitched his voice high. "Not the hole, not the hole, not that hole."

Dunk grabbed a piece of paper and wadded it up, tossing it at Wig. Of course, he missed, and they all laughed, even Dunk. It was nice having someone who got along with their group. The Navy had sent a few guys out as fill-ins while they reviewed men to fill the position full-time, but they hadn't always connected like they gelled with Dunk. Humor was a weird thing. Sometimes it clicked right away, and other times people took offense. He trusted the SEALs the Navy had sent them, but he liked that he could trust Dunk and they could laugh together.

He said goodbye to his friends before heading home. It was the day before Christmas, and for the first time in a while, excitement pinged through him. He hadn't bought anything expensive, but he hoped

Audrey liked his gift. Having a kid in his house on Christmas also added to the excitement. Meredith wasn't his, but he felt like she was. If Audrey and Meredith left, it would destroy him.

Christmas morning, they woke late, and Meredith opened her gifts. She was excited about everything, even the socks her mother purchased. He couldn't believe how fun Meredith was. She really just enjoyed life, and it made him appreciate everything more, too.

After they finished with Meredith's presents and she'd gone to her room to play with them, Audrey met him in the kitchen, both hands behind her back. "I have something for you."

His lips quirked up, and he grabbed the box from his pocket. "And I have something for you."

She handed him a box about nine inches long by six or something like that. It wasn't huge, but it had some weight. He wasn't expecting anything from her, and he certainly wasn't expecting something this big.

"You first," Audrey said.

Legs tore open the wrapping paper as excitement filled him. He glanced up, smiling at her before opening the box. He stared at the item, shocked to find a paperback copy of a book he really wanted. It

was from an admiral he admired. "This is amazing."
He opened the cover and saw the admiral's
signature. "How did you get it signed?"

Audrey's lips spread into a huge smile. "He came
into the store with his wife and kids. They were
shopping for shirts, and I'd just bought the book the
day before so I still had it under the counter at work.
When I saw him, I pulled it out from behind the
counter and held it up to check the photo on the
back of the jacket. He recognized the book
immediately and came over. I told him about you.
About how you were helping me. He said you
sounded like a real Navy man, someone he would be
proud to serve with."

Legs shook his head. "I can't believe you knew
how much this would mean to me. It's like..." Legs
met her gaze, and she saw moisture in his eyes right
before he pulled her into a hug. He held on for a long
moment, kissing the side of her head before letting
go. "I'm amazed."

He loved how her cheeks turned pink and the
way her smile radiated. A part of him was glad
neither of them felt comfortable getting into a sexual
relationship. He liked being her friend. He wanted
her to see him as valuable for more than just sex.
She'd been right when she said this was better. They

had a special connection he felt would last. Maybe they wouldn't get married and stay together for fifty years, but they were building a solid foundation.

"Open yours," Legs whispered.

Audrey tore open the paper then opened the box, tears filling her eyes. She reached for him and tugged him close as tears spilled down her cheeks.

"You remembered."

"It was important to you."

A sob escaped Audrey's lips as she pulled back and looked at the necklace. It wasn't exactly like what she'd lost in the fire, but it was as close as he could get to the photo she'd showed him of the necklace. She'd only talked about it a few times, but based on how she looked after she'd spoken about it, he knew it really was important to her.

"Thank you. When I lost that birthstone necklace, I felt like I had lost a piece of my soul. Can you help me put it on?"

"Sure." The clasp was tiny, but he managed to help her get the necklace on. "There you go."

She turned and pulled him in for another hug. It felt amazing being in her arms. He closed his eyes and imagined for a moment they were free to love each other. He wanted her with him next year and the next. He liked making Audrey happy, and from the book she'd bought him, it seemed like she enjoyed making him happy, too.

"I'm hungry," Meredith said from the den.

Audrey laughed as she moved out of his arms. "Sure, honey. How about some eggs?"

"I don't like them runny."

"We'll do scrambled," Legs said.

"Are you making them?" Meredith asked.

Legs nodded, and she sighed, then smiled. He knew Meredith liked his eggs better than Audrey's eggs. It might just be because Meredith was old enough to want to push away from her mother and start building her own identity, or she really might not like the way Audrey made eggs. Either way, he was happy he had Meredith and Audrey in his life. Audrey added way more to his life than he ever thought any woman would. That he also got to experience Meredith was a bonus. He didn't want to imagine a life without them. Somehow, he would make sure they could stay and build a life with him, because now he knew the greatest Christmas present ever was Meredith and Audrey.

CHAPTER 18

Meredith didn't want to go to sleep after spending the day having fun with Tony, but Audrey could tell her daughter was exhausted. When she stepped out from Meredith's room, she'd been expecting to sit with Tony and maybe see if he was willing to kiss. Nothing more, just a kiss. They'd had such a great day, and she was ready to file for divorce, even if it meant she had to go back to the mainland for a few months.

She stepped into the den and saw Tony dressed to head into work. "What's going on? I didn't think you had to work."

He shook his head. "Sorry. This is the bad part of being involved with a SEAL. I mean, I know we're not involved yet, but this could have happened last night. I can't tell you where I'm going or when I'll be back. Rawlins knows we're headed out, and he'll keep an eye on you. You have numbers for Jenna and the other women, right?"

She nodded as worry blossomed. "I know you have no say in whether you stay or go. I'm fine with it, or I will be." Audrey waved both hands in the air and rolled her eyes. "What I'm trying to say is I'll be here waiting for you."

He held her gaze for a long moment, then gave a sharp nod. "I'll come home to you."

Meredith would be unhappy, but this was part of it all. She couldn't tell Meredith much, but she would help her understand that Tony would return in a few weeks, and life wasn't changing.

At least Audrey hoped it wouldn't change. She poured a glass of wine and stepped out into the backyard. The stars were bright, and she said a prayer for Tony and his crew. Worry filled her, but she trusted Tony. He was strong and could take on whatever came his way.

The next few days with Meredith were difficult. Her daughter didn't understand why Tony had to leave or why Audrey had no idea when he would be back. Audrey thought about canceling her evening out with Liz and the other women, but Liz talked her into going.

Meredith seemed excited to spend the evening with Brooke and David. She was glad her daughter had a friend. She knew the months of hotel hopping, going from one city to the next had been hard on her.

The sitter was nineteen and had been watching kids for years. Audrey felt a little weird about leaving Meredith with someone so young, but Liz assured her everything would be okay.

It had been ages since Audrey had gone out for fun with other women. The first place they stopped was a restaurant. They sat in the bar area and ordered appetizers and drinks. Audrey stayed quiet, but she wasn't having a bad time. Cindy and Elle had known each other for years. They'd met Liz a few times when they'd all lived in Florida, but Liz said they were only acquaintances until they moved here.

Cindy pulled out her phone and held it up as she pointed at her and Liz. "You two, lean in, and I'll post you on my Insta page."

Audrey moved fast and ducked her head, covering her face with her hands. "Sorry, no photos."

"What is wrong with you?" Cindy asked. "First at school and now this. It's just a photo."

Audrey didn't want to tell the truth and worried that a lie would only make things worse. "I just can't."

"You think you're too special," Cindy pressed.

"No. I just…"

The woman rolled her eyes and held up her phone, so the screen faced Audrey. "Too late. I already put your photo up with your daughter on Insta and Facebook."

"Oh my God. Take it down." Fear filled Audrey. She couldn't believe someone would do that to her.

Cindy huffed. "I'm not taking it down. It's my photo."

Panic filled Audrey, leaving her feeling uneasy. "You have to. Please. He's insane. He'll come here and…" She couldn't say the words. It was too much to reveal to these women. She'd had misgivings about tonight, and maybe she shouldn't have come.

"Hey, are you okay?"

Audrey turned to see Jenna and Ashley, their foreheads wrinkled in concern. What could she tell them? They didn't know the whole story. They weren't really friends. They'd only met one time.

Audrey blew out a breath and turned to face Cindy. "I know it sounds petty, but you have to take my photo off social media. He will come here, and it will be bad if he finds us."

Cindy rolled her eyes and started to put her phone away, but Jenna grabbed it from her and opened Facebook, swiping through the photos.

"You can't do that," Cindy said.

Jenna hit her with a hard stare. "You can't load photos of people to social media without their permission."

"I told you no photos that day at the school party." Tears spilled down Audrey's cheeks. She didn't know what to do. Meredith could be in harm's way. She gasped and grabbed Liz's arm. "The kids. Call the sitter and make sure she has the alarm on."

"Shit. Do you think he would hurt my kids?" Worry spread over Liz's face.

"You're overreacting," Cindy rolled her eyes again as she waved her hand dismissively.

Audrey didn't like this Cindy chick. Anger flashed hot, and she opened her mouth, not thinking before speaking. "He blew up a hotel because he thought I was inside. Luckily I was gone for the day."

Cindy's eyes narrowed as she frowned. "You're overreacting."

"No, you're being a jerk," Jenna said as she handed the phone back to Cindy. "I deleted the photos and removed it from your phone. Don't take another photo of anyone and place it on social media without permission. If I find out you've done it again, I'll make sure you regret your actions." Jenna turned to Audrey. "Do you want a ride home?"

"Yes, please. I need to get Meredith."

Liz slung her purse over her shoulder. "I'm headed home now. I'll drive you."

"Don't go home," Jenna said. "Send me the address where you're picking up Meredith. I'll come get you, and you can spend the night at my place."

"I don't want to put you out," Audrey said.

Jenna waved off her worries. "Please, like I'd let you stay on your own after this. Until we have determined what damage was done—" Jenna shot Cindy a scornful look. "You're staying with me."

Audrey reached for Jenna and gave her a quick hug. She left with Liz, angry that Cindy had put her photo up.

"I'm sorry about that," Liz said.

"It's okay. If we hadn't gone to the restaurant with them, I wouldn't have known Cindy had snapped my photo and put it up on social media."

"Is it your ex?" Liz asked.

All Audrey could do was nod. She didn't want to explain that she was still married to the jerk. How would she explain this to anyone? It was so freaking complicated. She couldn't believe she'd told Cindy that Eddy had blown up her hotel. She prayed Cindy didn't mention that to anyone else.

"Do you think he'll come here and try to do something?" Liz's voice shook with fear.

Audrey shrugged. "I have no clue what he'll do. I'm glad the kids are out of school for another week. This will give us time to see if he found the photo."

Liz pulled into her driveway and cut the engine. "Text me tomorrow."

A car approached, and Audrey froze until she saw Jenna behind the wheel. "I'll keep you updated."

"Thanks. And Audrey, I wish you would have told me. I would have been on the lookout for your photo. I'd seen the picture and thought maybe you'd allowed Cindy to put it up. I'm sorry. I should have told you."

Audrey reached over and hugged Liz. "Thank you. I'm just embarrassed about it all."

"Don't be. Trust me, there are things we all put up with and—" Liz blew out a breath. "I'll tell you later. Like once you get your stuff solved."

A weird feeling slid through Audrey. She should ask Liz what was going on, but she needed to get

Meredith. "Sure. And if you need anything, don't hesitate."

Liz laughed. "You are too nice. Here you are worried about someone who might come after you, and you're offering to help me. I'm fine. My worries are small compared to yours."

They got out of the car and headed into Liz's house. Meredith was disappointed they had to leave but happy they were going to Jenna's house. Audrey felt odd about staying with Jenna, but she didn't want to sleep alone at Tony's place. For now, she would need to keep her head down and wait. She hated the wait because Eddy had always been good at getting revenge slowly.

CHAPTER 19

Audrey slept in the guest room in the same bed as Meredith. It had been a few months since she'd slept in the same bed with her daughter and was woken up when Meredith kicked her side. Audrey decided it was time to get some coffee.

Jenna was in the kitchen, already pouring up a cup of coffee. Guilt slid through Audrey.

"I didn't wake you, did I?"

"No, not at all. My little princess likes a bottle at five in the morning. She's back asleep and will probably stay that way until seven."

"I forgot how difficult life was with a baby."

Jenna handed over a mug. "She's a good baby, but it does take time."

"Will you have more?" Audrey asked.

Jenna's lips twisted into a frown. "No. I can't."

"Oh, I'm sorry."

"It's okay. I love Lila, and if we decide we want more, we can adopt."

"I love Meredith, but I made sure I wouldn't get pregnant with a second baby with Eddy. I honestly thought I could divorce him, but that's a joke."

"Want to tell me what has been going on?"

Audrey settled on the loveseat, and Jenna sat beside her. She should have found time to tell Jenna what had happened with Eddy before now. She'd almost told them at Thanksgiving, but Meredith had begged her to see the dolphin. At the time, Audrey felt relief. Now she wished they all knew.

She sipped her coffee as she related the story, all the sordid details, even the hotel blowing up and how she'd held Tony at gunpoint.

"Of course, Tony took the gun away from me so fast I thought he might kill me."

Jenna chuckled. "Yeah, they're fast and strong. I'm glad you didn't shoot him."

"Same. I can't believe I thought I could do this on my own."

"I'll check with some of my sources and see what they have on Eddy."

Audrey stared at Jenna, her eyebrows raised. "Are you military, too?"

Jenna shook her head. "No, but I worked in the government. I have access to people who have access to information. We'll make sure you're safe before we send you home."

"I fear what he'll do to the school if he figures out where that photo was taken."

"Do you think he would harm everyone there?"

Audrey shrugged. "If he thought I was inside, maybe. I need to know if he's coming here. Maybe he didn't see the photo, but I can't know for sure."

"You know you're staying here at our house until the guys get back unless we get confirmation you're safe."

"I don't know when that would be. I mean, if he sends someone I don't know, how would we know?"

Jenna frowned. "He could contract with someone over here."

Audrey blew out a harsh breath. "I hate that my photo was up on the internet. I've been so careful."

Jenna took a sip of her coffee then shook her head. "When the senator flew to Hawaii to kidnap me, I wasn't expecting it."

"Wait, what? A senator tried to kidnap you?"

Jenna's chuckle surprised Audrey. She took

another sip of her coffee as she watched Jenna out of the corner of her eyes.

"Sorry, I forgot you didn't know. The branch of the government I worked for was investigating Senator Devlin—"

Audrey held up her hand. "Wait, didn't he end up in jail or something? I remember something about a senator, but I don't remember it all."

"Devlin is gone. I don't know if it was my friend or a foe, but someone in prison killed him. They never found out who."

Audrey blew out a breath. "I'm glad you're safe."

"Same. And I want to make sure you're safe. If something happens, we'll deal with it, but we shouldn't go looking for trouble."

"Thank you," Audrey said.

Jenna flashed her a smile. "Of course. We're friends."

"I'm not dating Tony, you know that, right?"

Jenna nodded. "He likes you, though."

Audrey gave a heavy sigh. "I know. I just can't start something with this dark cloud hanging over my head."

Jenna sipped her coffee. "If you were free, would you want to be with Tony?"

Audrey nodded. "Very much. I'd like to be with

him now, but I can't force him to be with me while I'm still legally married to Eddy."

"Are you trying to get a divorce?"

Audrey's head started aching as well as her chest. "I want one, but I'm afraid of what he'll do."

"With a daughter in the mix, I can understand why you're worried."

Sadness hit Audrey hard. She'd made so many mistakes. "I never should have married him."

Jenna reached out and patted her shoulder. "You know, there're loads of things we never should have done that we can regret or get past and move on." Jenna stood. "So today, one of the food kitchens is having a huge meal giveaway. We're all meeting this morning and going to work. The kids will be there, and we'll take turns watching them. Why don't you go shower, and we'll get ready to leave?"

Audrey swallowed as worry took over. "Are you sure it's okay for me to be there?"

"Yes. Some SEALs will be there, not all of them, but it's not only the women helping. There'll be plenty of protection along with some of the women who I call friends."

Audrey nodded though she felt a little odd about going. "They won't be weird about the fact I'm not dating Tony, right?"

"They don't care. As long as you're nice to him, they'll be fine."

Audrey nodded before heading to the bathroom. Meredith woke up about thirty minutes before they were set to leave. She seemed excited to meet new people. Audrey wished she felt the same.

About an hour into the task, Audrey realized she'd been silly to worry. There were so many people who were nice. She was working beside Elodie, Mustang, and Lexie. She'd met Kenna, Pid, Jag, and Slate. She already knew Ashley and Sunshine.

The building they were in wasn't in the nicest area of downtown, but with the guys there, she felt safe. No one asked if she was dating Tony. Instead, they just accepted that she was Jenna's friend.

"I heard you were new to Hawaii," Elodie said.

Lexie handed her a bun, and Audrey began preparing the sandwich. "I am. I arrived in October."

"Do you like it?" Lexie asked.

She nodded. "It's nice."

Mustang wrapped the sandwich she'd made, placing it along with the others they were planning to hand out. "You haven't seen much, though."

She glanced at him and shook her head. "No. I need a vehicle."

"Hey," Slate called out. "One of the guys I know has a car, and he doesn't want to ship it back to the States. It's not new and has been passed around to about five different owners here in Hawaii."

Audrey shrugged. "I don't know. I don't have much money."

Slate chuckled. "It's not going to be expensive. Honestly, he might be willing to make a deal. I'll pass the information on to Legs."

Audrey nodded, not wanting to mention that she wasn't with Legs and would be making her own decision. It was easier to just stay silent.

Jenna cleared her throat and met Slate's gaze. "You know, Audrey can make her mind up on her own."

Slate narrowed his eyes. "I just didn't want to butt in on Legs' woman."

Heat filled Audrey. Now she would have to reveal how she was using Tony. "We aren't together."

"What?" Slate narrowed his eyes as he stared at her.

"He's just a friend. I'm not his girlfriend, and we're not dating. He's a good guy who offered to help when my life got to be too much."

"Wait, he's letting you get away?" Pid asked.

She shook her head. "I'm not—he's not letting

anything happen," Audrey huffed. "I'm just in a bad place, and he's helping."

"Guys, give her a break," Mustang said. "Elodie and I can go with you to look at the vehicle. I can look at the engine if you need help with the mechanics."

"Don't listen to Slate," Kenna said. "You can be a strong woman and don't need a man."

Audrey's eyes grew hot as she fixed another sandwich. First, Tony had been so kind, then Jenna and her friends, and now Elodie and Mustang were offering to help. Kenna was encouraging her. If these people got any nicer, she would bawl her eyes out.

"Hey, are you okay?" Elodie asked.

She swiped at her eyes with the back of her hand. "Yeah, it's just I can't believe so many of you are nice. I don't deserve this, and yet you all are treating me like I'm one of you, but I'm an outsider."

"Hey," Pid said as he walked past. "You're not an outsider. You're here, so you're a part of our family. We take care of family. There's a reason Legs is helping you, so we're going to help you, too."

Audrey glanced around, seeing that it was still just their group in the back room where they were preparing the food. Ashley had the kids in another room, keeping them busy as the rest of them worked. Audrey cleared her throat and tried not to hide too much as she spoke.

"My husband—I ran before I could get a divorce—I guess he's a part of the mob. I saw him kill someone. I thought he was going to kill me next. I took off and have been on the run for a few months. He could come after me and kill me. If you're around me, then you might be collateral damage."

"I say bring it," Pid said. "If he wants a fight, I'll give him one."

"I'll take him down," Aleck said.

The other guys echoed Pid and Aleck's words. Worry spread through her.

"I told you these people were good," Jenna said.

"But I don't want any of you getting hurt," Audrey said.

"Don't worry about us. We have some special people keeping watch over Eddy and his crew. If they head this way, we'll know," Mustang said.

"So you know about that?" Audrey asked.

"I talked to Legs. He's a good man. Just remember that once you're free."

Audrey nodded, afraid to say too much. She didn't know if Tony would want her, much less what kind of relationship they would have. Maybe he didn't want to be strapped down with kids and a wife who had issues.

An alarm rang on someone's phone, and Jenna pulled her phone out. "My time to watch the kids. I'll send Ashley out."

Since Meredith was older, the other women told Audrey she didn't need to help out with the kids. They were fine hanging out with the babies because Meredith helped them with bottles and grabbed diapers for the babies. She was glad Meredith liked babies so much. Meredith had always been an easy kid. If only Eddy had been a decent person, but if he had been, she never would have met Tony.

She wanted different things now. Maybe she wouldn't develop a relationship with Tony, but they might have something special in time. For now, she needed to concentrate on staying alive.

CHAPTER 20

Legs saw the muzzle flash from the incoming shot and ducked behind a wall. The person on the other end of that gun wasn't a good shot, but they were getting closer. He needed to find an escape soon.

He'd been cut off from his team, forced to head down an alley and away from their exfil location. They wouldn't leave him behind, that he was sure of, but he hated the position he'd found himself in.

Legs slipped down another alley and found an open door. He debated about two seconds before he slipped inside. He heard no one. Maybe they'd slipped out, or perhaps this was actually an abandoned building. For now, he would use it to hide.

One minute passed, then two. He waited for anyone to come and find him. Nothing happened.

After ten minutes, Legs finally blew out a breath of relief. He found a place to sit and inspect his leg. The wound was deep, and he probably needed stitches which he didn't have time for. Instead he slapped a seal on, hoping his leg wasn't too messed up.

He ignored the pain as he hydrated, checked his gun and ammunition, then headed out. He needed to meet up with his crew. Being in the wind sucked. The main part of their mission went well, but then everything fell apart.

Legs ran down one alley to another. He knew roughly where he could meet up with his team, but the buildings had blocked his view of the horizon. He checked his compass again, deciding he was going the right way.

He slowed as he came to a road, knowing it would be dangerous to cross. The hair on the back of his neck stood on end. Someone was watching.

Legs eased back, hiding in the shadows of the building. He checked up high then low, searching for the source of his unease.

His stomach tightened, and he was ready to step into the street when the wall beside him exploded.

Legs ducked fast and then moved in the other direction. He didn't want to think about what would have happened if he'd gone out into the street like he'd planned. That had been close.

He didn't know where to go next. The enemy knew where he was now, or had an idea. He had to get out of this section of the city, or they'd find and kill him. The empty building where he'd rested was too close to where he'd almost been shot. He had to find a different place to hunker down.

The moon would rise in twenty or thirty minutes, and then it would be easier to spot him. The enemy had the advantage since there were more of them, and they knew the area. He wasn't in his element. Maybe he wouldn't make it out this time.

Static crackled on his headset. "Six, this is one."

"Go ahead," Legs said.

"We're close to you if you're hearing this."

Relief flooded him, but he couldn't relax yet. If he lost his edge, he could lose his life. "It's about time you boys found me."

"Can you move?"

Vine's question hit him in the gut. "I'm good. Just need a place to go."

Location coordinates were given, and he started making his way to the place he would meet up with his team. He no longer felt defeated. Instead, Legs moved with confidence. Each alley was a new possibility of being shot, but he kept his head on straight and watched everything.

He was about a block away when two guys pinned him down with gunfire. There was no way he could get out of this. He needed a miracle. If he backed up, he would be in the open for about three seconds. If he stayed where he was, these two would eventually hit him. If he ran at them, he would go down.

Legs decided he had to take them out. He couldn't get out of this without taking a chance. Then he heard more gunfire. When he heard someone call his name after the gunfire ceased, joy filled him.

His team had found him, and they were getting out. They still had to fight their way out of the city, but they made it. The trek to the exfil location took another hour, but soon enough, he was on a helicopter, thanking his lucky stars that he had a great team.

"I thought you were a goner," Dunk said as he patted Legs on the shoulder.

Legs grunted. "Same. When we got separated, I thought I was dead."

"I swore you got hit," Wig said.

"I did. It's not bad, just a scratch. A few inches over, and you all would have been carrying my dead ass home."

"Shit," Vine said as he wiped his hand over his face. "Too close for me. I didn't like that."

"We had fun, though, right?" Legs said.

"Right," Minx said as he thumped Legs on the shoulder. "How bad is your leg?"

"Not bad. It hurts like a bitch, but what doesn't hurt after a mission like that?"

"You're going to sickbay as soon as we land," Vine said.

Legs grunted and then shook his head. "Shit."

They flew in low, landing on an aircraft carrier. He moved to climb out of the chopper, but the adrenaline spiking his blood had worn off, and the pain was too much. He hopped a few steps then Vine and Wig caught him under the arms and threatened to carry him on a stretcher if he didn't let them help.

Once in with the doctor, he was allowed to remove his pants instead of having them cut off. He laid back on the bed, his mind on Audrey and Meredith. He needed her to start the divorce proceedings. She needed to be rid of the jerk and be free to move on, even if she wanted to move on with someone else.

His stomach churned. If something had happened to him, Audrey would have been out of luck with nowhere to go. Maybe she didn't want to be his wife, but he wanted her to have the choice. Once he got home, he would make it very clear he was interested in a relationship.

The doctor cleaned his wound, shaking his head the whole time. "You're lucky," the doctor said for the fifth or maybe sixth time.

"Or maybe it was skill," Legs said.

The doc shook his head. "Nope. This is luck. I'm glad you're not dead. I hate having to sign death certificates."

Legs grunted. "I bet that's a bummer."

The doctor nodded then cut the thread he'd used to sew Legs up. "You should heal in a few weeks. You're going to be sore. You'll need to see the doctor on base to get released to work."

"Ugh, I don't want to be sidelined."

"Tough cookies. When you play in the sandbox that you guys play in, someone's bound to get hurt. You and your guys did great out there. You'll get some time to relax, and then you can come back and kick another ass, but for now, you're going to rest."

Legs chuckled. "I'll be back out there kicking ass in no time."

The doctor growled. "I never want to see you again. Unless it's on a golf course or at dinner. Stay healthy, and don't get shot again."

The doctor finished up and stepped away. A nurse cleaned up the area before allowing Legs to get dressed.

He met his team in the canteen and slowly lowered to the seat, groaning on the way down. He'd refused heavy pain meds and gone with over-the-counter stuff. It hadn't taken the bite away, but it dulled the pain a bit.

"You all stitched up?" Vine asked.

Legs nodded. "Sure am."

Vine lifted his chin. "Eat something, then we're heading out."

"I'll get you a tray." Wig hopped up but stopped and turned back to the table. "Want anything special?"

"Hot food would be good."

Wig came back minutes later with some beef and chicken that looked amazing, along with some vegetables and mashed potatoes. He sighed as he ate, glad he'd survived.

"If I'd died, would you all have buried me with

mashed potatoes?"

Vine rolled his eyes. "Just eat. We need to go."

Legs finished the meal and stopped by the showers to get cleaned up. The doctor had set him up with a waterproof bandage that would need to be changed out once he got back to Hawaii, but for now, the bandage meant he could shower.

They were heading to a base in Japan, then they'd be flying home. In the quiet space on the plane, he had time to think hard about Audrey. She'd come into his life at an interesting time. They had decisions that had to be made, and he just hoped they made the right ones.

CHAPTER 21

Audrey hadn't heard anything from Rawlins or Mustang. As far as she knew, Eddy hadn't figured out her location. She hated that someone had posted her photo. Cindy hadn't called or texted to apologize. She guessed Cindy had no remorse.

Audrey made dinner, using stuff from the back of the freezer that hadn't gone bad. She'd tossed a bag of frozen carrots that had so much frostbite they were dehydrated.

Jenna stepped into the kitchen and sighed. "She's out."

"That's good."

"Do you need any help?"

"I've got it covered. Almost everything I used was

from the back of the freezer. I hope you weren't saving that stuff."

Jenna squinched up her nose. "Nope. If it's back there, I've probably forgotten about it." She took a deep breath and sighed. "It smells so good."

"Thank you."

They were about to sit down when the door opened. Audrey's head whipped around as fear filled her. But there was no reason to fear. Vine and Tony stepped in. It only took her a second to see Tony's limp as he moved.

"What happened?" she asked as she drew closer.

"It's nothing," Tony said.

"He was shot," Vine said.

"What?" Audrey rushed over, touching his face, making sure he was okay. Tears formed in her eyes.

Tony reached up and wiped one tear off her cheek. "I'm okay. It was just a graze."

"He's lucky," Vine said.

Audrey wrapped her arms around Tony and held on as tears ran down her cheeks. She held on, not wanting to let go.

"I'm really okay," Tony said.

"What smells so good," Vine asked.

"Come eat," Jenna said. "There's plenty in the pan."

"Are you hungry?" Audrey asked Tony.

"Oh yeah, I could eat."

They settled around the table, talking about nothing important. She glanced up at one point and noticed Tony watching her. She smiled, wondering what he was thinking. A look in Tony's eyes made her want to spend more time with him. She couldn't believe he'd been shot. It really was time to end this thing with Eddy so she could move on. Maybe Tony didn't want her forever, but she needed to give them the option of exploring what they meant to each other.

After eating, Vine asked Audrey to sit in the den and talk. She felt like whatever he was going to say was serious.

"Listen, I heard from Rawlins. None of Eddy's guys nor Eddy have headed this way. I don't want you to let down your guard, but if they found your image out there, they don't know where you are."

Audrey didn't react for a moment. "Are we safe to go home?"

Vine nodded. "Rawlings has been watching your house. No one has come by. With Legs there, even with him injured, I feel comfortable saying you can go home."

Audrey blew out the breath she'd been holding. "Thank you."

Vine smiled. "We're happy to help. We're staying on this."

Audrey nodded. "I want to file for divorce."

Tony let out an explosive breath. "Thank goodness." His eyes went wide, and he reached for her hand. "Sorry, I'm just glad you're going to be moving on."

She squeezed his hand. "I'm afraid of what he'll do."

"We get that," Vine said. "You'll have people here to help keep you safe."

"He's going to be pissed."

Tony pulled her close and gave her a hug. "I'm sure he will be, but you're going to be okay."

Audrey didn't know what to think. After hugging Jenna and thanking her for the hospitality, Tony said he could carry Meredith out to his vehicle, but Vine said he'd do it. Vine followed them to Tony's place and got Meredith into her bed without waking her.

Once Audrey was sure Meredith wasn't going to wake up, she moved to Tony's room and found him wearing only his underwear. Heat crept up her chest as she noticed the muscles on his shoulders and back. She let her gaze trail down his body to his incredible legs. The bandage on his thigh was a stark contrast to his tanned skin. The desire to reach out and touch him grew. Her heart kicked into high gear. She shouldn't be here. Audrey turned to leave, but Legs reached out and grabbed her hand.

"Don't go."

"I—" slowly she turned to look at him, and her eyes dipped low, taking in his chest and lower to his belly where a little trail of hair disappeared under the band of his underwear. "Oh God, I'm so—"

He pulled her into a hug. "After I got shot and everything calmed down enough for me to think, I realized I can't let this go unsaid. I know you're still married to Eddy, and I'm not going to encourage you to do anything. But I need you to know that as soon as you're free, I want to date you."

Audrey felt like the pressure was too much, and laughter spilled out. Tony narrowed his eyes, and she leaned in, brushing her lips over his. They both gasped.

"Sorry. I just can't believe you got shot, and you were thinking of me. I feel like there's this weight sitting on top of my head, and I can't deal with it. It's so much pressure, and then you were shot, and my photo was posted on social media, and I couldn't handle any of it, so I had to sleep at Jenna's house. I didn't mean to laugh but—"

He pulled her closer, and her hands landed on his pecs. A gasp escaped her lips.

"It's okay. I get why you laughed. The last few days have been stressful. Yes, I was shot, but I'm okay. We can talk about the photo later."

She glanced up and saw caring shining in his eyes. No question, she could get lost in his gaze. He had been so kind, so caring, and this was the first time they'd been this close for this long. She didn't want to ever let him go.

"I almost don't want to know who posted your photo."

Audrey shrugged and rolled her eyes. "I don't even really know her. I'd told her no photos, and then she took one in secret."

Tony's eyes grew darker. "That sucks. Why are people like that?"

She should step back, but she didn't want to. Desire filled her, leaving her needing more of Tony. Her hands had slipped from his pecs to his sides, and she was contemplating moving her hands lower when Meredith called for her.

"Mommy, Mommy, where are you?"

Audrey sighed. "Sorry."

"It's okay," Tony said before he lightly brushed his lips over her forehead and then took a step back.

Audrey couldn't stop herself from taking him all in. She noticed the bulge in his underwear, and her throat went dry. She'd only ever had sex with Eddy, and it had been okay—well, boring. She bet sex with Tony wouldn't be boring.

After getting Meredith to use the bathroom and getting her back in bed, she waited for her daughter's breathing to even out before leaving her room. Audrey wanted to search for Tony, but she moved to the bathroom and brushed her teeth. She should get some sleep. Tony wasn't going anywhere, and she had some decisions that needed to be made. Divorcing Eddy would be tough, but she had to get out from under his thumb.

CHAPTER 22

New Year's Eve came and went. They settled back
into their routine. Audrey hadn't come back to his
room that night, and though he'd wanted her in his
arms, he knew she needed to wait until her divorce
was final.

His leg healed but was still a little achy if he did
too much. He was back on active status but still
doing some physical therapy to work out the last bit
of soreness.

The physical therapist had just finished
massaging his leg when he got a text. He checked his
messages, seeing a smiley face and what looked like
an upside-down horn with stuff coming out of the
top. Then he saw the little three dots indicating that
Audrey was typing.

"Good news?" the physical therapist asked.

He shrugged. "Maybe."

The guy stepped back as he put away the tool he'd been using and grabbed one of the towels he'd used. "Well, I have good news for you about your leg. You're almost there. You need to keep moving, and you should probably invest in a percussive therapy massager for that area, but your movement is good. I think one more session, and you'll be done."

"Awesome. Thanks, man."

The guy gave him a fist bump and stepped away. Legs checked his messages again, his breath stalling for a second as he read the words. Audrey had filed. Eddy would get the paperwork in the next few days.

His skin prickled, and his lungs felt way too small. They were stepping into danger. Legs still had her old phone and had checked it a few times, but it had been a while since he'd turned on the device. He needed to check it and figure out what was going on.

Vine called as he headed out to his vehicle. "What's up?" Tony asked as he answered.

"Tomorrow morning, do you think you'd be good for a hike? Nothing big, the women and kids would be coming."

"Sure. Let me make sure Audrey is free."

"Awesome. Seven in the morning, and I'll shoot you the address."

"Sounds great."

He ended the call and dialed Audrey. When she answered, his balls pulled up tight. She made him want so much more from life. He couldn't believe he'd ever thought finding a woman at a club for sex would ever be enough. He wanted Audrey and Meredith in his life.

"Vine called and wanted to know if we could join them for a hike tomorrow?"

"Yes. I think that would be great. Meredith would love it."

"What would I love?" Meredith's tiny voice over the phone brought a smile to his lips. He loved that child. She made everything better.

"Going on a hike with the team."

"Yes!" Meredith shouted.

He chuckled, happiness filling him. "I'll be there in a few minutes. I just finished with physical therapy."

"Dinner is ready. Want to eat outside on the patio?"

"Yes. But anywhere is good as long as it's with you."

Audrey sucked in a breath. "You make me feel too good saying things like that."

"You should feel good. I'll be there in a few."

He hung up, wondering how long it would be before they started dating. Like really being together. He knew they needed to wait for a bit since she'd be going through a divorce, but he hoped they could start getting serious soon.

It would be weird dating her since they lived together. Thinking of being with Audrey was making his cock hard, and they still had to eat dinner. He turned his mind to work and the things he had to do in the next week. His locker needed to be cleaned out. At some point, they would go on a long run and do the obstacle course. His legs were almost at one hundred percent. He was getting older, and getting shot highlighted the little things like his back aching more, along with how he felt older when he got up in the morning. Maybe that feeling would leave with the pain in his thigh, if the pain in his thigh ever left.

Meredith came running at him when he stepped into his house, flinging herself into his arms. He laughed as he picked her up, kissing her cheek.

"How was today?" Legs asked.

Meredith started a rundown of her day, telling

him about the way one of her friends had punched a boy.

"Oh, she shouldn't have punched him."

"But he grabbed her ponytail and tugged her backward. She almost fell, so she punched him."

Legs didn't like this story. It made him angry and want to punish the kid who'd pulled the girl's hair. But he was just a kid, and the impulse to go off on him was wrong.

He controlled his anger as he spoke. "It's not right to tug on someone else's hair. That boy should be punished."

Meredith nodded. "He is now. All the girls sat down and wouldn't move until the teacher listened to us. We almost got detention, but finally, another teacher came up and listened."

"Really?" Where had Meredith learned to stage a sit-in? He needed to talk to Audrey and determine what she thought about all this.

"Yes. He has detention now."

"That's good. I'm glad he is getting punished, too."

"He said he was going to hit us all."

"Wait, what?" Legs wanted to go down to the school and have a chat with the kid. He blew out a breath, trying to release the anger.

"Don't worry about it," Audrey said as she stepped into the den. "I had a chat with her teacher. The boy's parents are being talked to, and he's being kept in alternative school until he can receive counseling."

"Wow. I don't even know what to say."

"I want to go outside and look at the flowers," Meredith said.

"Let me change, and I'll be out there in a few." Legs headed to his room as Meredith and Audrey slipped outside.

Dinner smelled great. Living with Audrey was great. He hadn't believed it would be this good. He wished he'd known Meredith when she was a baby, but he was glad he was getting a chance to know her now. She was a breath of fresh air in his day. She made him feel better about the future of the world. Working as a SEAL, seeing all kinds of crap had left him feeling a little off. For a while, after some bad shit he saw his first year as a SEAL, he'd wondered if it was worth trying to save humanity. Now he knew it was. There were some very bad people out there, but so many more wonderful people he never interacted with. The boy who had threatened her needed some help, but most of the kids in her class seemed good.

He grabbed the food from the oven and plated his portion and Audrey's before he stuck his head out the door and got Audrey's attention. "Has Meredith eaten?"

"She had a sandwich earlier." Audrey turned to her daughter and asked her a question. "She'll eat off my plate if she's hungry."

"Okay. I'll be out in just a minute."

Seconds later, Audrey was in the kitchen, grabbing glasses of water for them to drink. She'd left the back door open so they could hear Meredith.

"Let's talk later," Legs said.

Audrey nodded, her lips curving up in a smile. Though she probably dreaded what Eddy would do, she seemed excited. Getting rid of the weight of Eddy would be good for Audrey. Already she was happier, and the divorce wasn't final. He could imagine how good their lives would be once the divorce was final and Eddy was out of their lives.

Meredith was asleep by eight-thirty, and Audrey joined him outside on the patio. They'd left the door open a crack so they could hear Meredith if she woke up.

"Are you nervous?" Legs asked.

"Yes, but excited. I can't wait to be free from him. I know there will be a fight, but I'm glad I started the paperwork. Maybe he'll just let me go. I'm not asking for child support. I just want to be rid of him."

Legs sipped his beer, watching the stars as he mulled over the potential problems. Eddy had no clue where Audrey was staying, but he might figure it out. They would need to be vigilant, but he didn't think she needed to hide at home.

"You're frowning. What are you thinking?"

He turned to face her, wishing they were at the point he could lean over and kiss her, then carry her to his bed. For a moment, he thought about lying to her. He didn't want to make her scared, but she needed to have a healthy amount of fear.

"Just security concerns."

Her eyebrows raised. "US security or my security?"

He took her hand and squeezed. "Your security. I don't know what he'll do. We do have the advantage that he doesn't know who I am or that we met. This house isn't in my name, and my aunt who owns the house has a different last name."

"That's good, I guess."

"He won't even know where to look for you. Just because you used an attorney in Honolulu doesn't mean you live on this island."

Audrey blew out a breath. "Since the attorney is part of a partner firm in New York, I'm not sure he'll even know I'm in Hawaii, at least not for a while. I just don't want Meredith to suffer. Running last year was tough on her. She's so much happier now."

"How about you? Are you happier?"

Audrey's lips curved up into a smile. "I am. And it's not just…"

He leaned in, wanting to get closer to her. "Not just what?"

It was too dark to see any blush on her cheeks, but the way she dipped her head made him think her cheeks were pink. He wished they were free to explore each other, but he didn't want to mess anything up for her with the pending divorce.

She made a noise that sounded almost like a grunt. "I like you. Okay? I've said it. I think it's obvious by the way I swoon after you, but yes, I like you. I want to be with you, but this thing with Eddy—"

He squeezed her hand. Desire ran through him, and he pushed it away. He wouldn't pull her onto his lap or kiss her like he wanted. She was trying hard to be good. She didn't need him being a jerk and taking advantage of her.

"I want to be with you, in a relationship with you."

"I feel the same."

"I wish I was free."

"You will be soon, and then we can start dating."

Audrey threw back her head, and laugher spilled out, sizzling along his nerves. She made him want things he had no business wanting yet.

"Don't you think since we're already living together, we can skip the dating part?"

He shook his head. "No way. I want to woo you into my arms and into my bed."

Audrey snorted. "You won't need to do much since I'm already there."

Her words made his dick hard. She wanted to be in his bed, and he wanted her there. What were they waiting for? Eddy sucked. The man was in his way. But they had to wait for the legal process to run its course. He kept hoping Eddy would want to end this fast and just give her the divorce, but deep down, he knew that probably wasn't going to happen. Eddy wasn't the type to go quietly into the night. The jerk would rage like an out-of-control gorilla and cause problems. They would have to wait this out.

CHAPTER 23

Excitement skated over Audrey's nerves as they parked in the lot and spied most of Tony's team. Meredith was already climbing out of her seat by the time Tony opened the door on his side. She ran over to Jenna and Ashley, asking about the babies.

Audrey stepped around the SUV, and Tony threw his arm over her shoulder. She looked up into his eyes, and a shiver worked through her. He didn't say anything, but he didn't need to. She saw the desire plain as day.

Tony dropped his arm and moved to the back of the vehicle, grabbing the pack to carry Meredith and a bag he'd packed with snacks. They still had their picnic lunch in yet another bag.

Audrey took the snack bag from Tony and

headed over to the women, hoping Meredith wasn't too much.

"Are there bears here?" Meredith asked Jenna.

Jenna shook her head. "No, no bears."

Vine stepped over and knelt so he was at eye level with Meredith. "There are a few animals we need to avoid, so if you want to touch something, ask one of us first."

Audrey lifted her eyebrows when Vine glanced up at her. "What animals?"

"A few centipedes, a caterpillar, snails," Tony said as he came over.

"That shouldn't be too bad," Audrey said.

"No, it's not. We just need to be aware and use our eyes and ears when we're out."

Tony smiled at Meredith. "Do you want to walk for a while or get in the pack?"

Meredith looked at the babies being carried by other men and shook her head. "I'll walk for a bit. I want to explore."

"Sounds good. I'll have the pack if you need to be carried."

Audrey liked this group of people. She didn't know them well, but she'd learned their names, and they accepted her.

The hike lasted about two hours. The guys

pointed out trees and bushes to Meredith, telling her what she could use to survive if she ever got lost in the jungle. Audrey wasn't sure the lesson was something she wanted Meredith learning, but her daughter was having a good time, and she walked the entire way. Audrey could tell by the way Meredith dragged her feet by the end that she was exhausted.

As they set up their food, Meredith rested her head on the picnic table. When Audrey came over to check on her, she found Meredith asleep. She didn't want to wake her daughter, so she kept her sandwich wrapped up and figured she could eat it later. The guys all smiled when they realized Meredith was asleep, and Tony moved to sit beside her.

They talked and laughed, joking with each other about things they'd done in the past. Everyone wanted Dunk to show off his skills at shooting trash into the trashcan. He rolled his eyes and grabbed five different pieces of trash, missing each time.

"But he can hit a target in the center at four hundred yards without fail," Wig said.

"That's different. It's easy to hit the target," Dunk said.

The women chuckled, and Audrey joined in, not feeling like such an outsider. She was getting closer to Jenna, Ashley, and Sunshine. They planned a girls' night out for the next Friday as long as the guys didn't have to work. They'd invited her, and at first, she was going to turn them down, but she decided she was being silly thinking they wouldn't want to spend time with her. They'd asked, so she said she would go.

Meredith woke up, her eyes squinched together as she rubbed her forehead then her cheek. "Why didn't you tell me it was time to eat?"

"Here, I have your sandwich," Audrey said.

"You can sit on my lap and eat if you want," Tony said.

"We're not going anywhere," Vine added. "Did you enjoy the hike?"

Meredith nodded as she took a bite of her sandwich. "I liked the waterfall we saw. It was big."

"It was," Tony said.

The guys chatted with Meredith about the hike, talking about the things they'd seen. They went over basic survival information, some of which Audrey didn't even know.

Meredith climbed off Tony's lap and came over, whispering in Audrey's ear. "Sure. I'll take you."

"Hold up," Tony said.

Both Audrey and Meredith turned to him. "I just need to check for animals."

"Oh," Audrey said.

Tony walked over with them, and then all the women came over, too. Jenna caught Audrey's eye and shrugged. "If someone is checking, I'm using the bathroom."

Tony and Vine ended up checking each toilet, making sure nothing was hanging out under the lids, and then declared the bathrooms clear.

Meredith went first then they took turns. The other women were excited about their night out. "Did you have a group of friends back in New York to go out with?" Sunshine asked.

Audrey shook her head. "No. Eddy wouldn't let me go out. I had a few friends, but we didn't see each other often."

"Oh, I'm sorry," Ashley said.

Audrey shrugged. "It's okay. I think my life will be getting better now."

"Yes, it will," Jenna said.

They came out of the bathroom, and Quirk, Wig, and Minx offered to play with Meredith. They all ran around the clearing by the parking lot, playing variations of chase and catch. By the time they left, it was close to noon. They were planning on meeting at the pool in Quirk's community. Audrey was looking forward to time in the pool.

The guys helped Meredith learn to swim better, and Audrey didn't have to worry about keeping her daughter safe. All the guys pitched in and took turns watching Meredith. Audrey felt like she'd actually had a pool day by the time they packed up for the evening.

"Did you have a good time?" Tony asked.

"I did. That was fun."

"It was great," Meredith said. She went on to detail everything she'd done with the guys.

Audrey was incredibly thankful she'd met Tony. She'd never known guys could be so good with kids or that they were so good in general.

By eight that evening, Meredith was in bed, fast asleep. Audrey had gotten her to take a shower and wash her hair, which was a miracle. She came into the den and plopped down on the couch.

"I'm exhausted."

Tony moved to sit beside her, holding her close. "Did you really have a good time today?"

She nodded but kept her eyes closed. "I did. Your friends are great."

"They like you, too."

"Is this how you all usually are? I mean when holiday stuff isn't happening?"

"Pretty much. We don't spend every weekend together, but we do enjoy being together."

"They seem like good people."

She felt Tony adjust and opened her eyes, turning so she could see him. He looked tired but sexy.

"Do you think this divorce will be easy?" Audrey asked.

He shook his head, remembering that he wanted to look at her latest messages. "He doesn't seem like a reasonable guy. I doubt he'll be decent during this. You'll just have to be patient and don't expect too much. It will take time, but we have time."

She laughed and leaned against him. "I feel like I both have time and don't. I don't want to lose you."

"I'm not going anywhere," Tony said.

Her gaze met his, and she saw the promise shining in his eyes. He was here to stay.

"I hate that I didn't know you before."

He cupped her face and leaned his forehead against hers. "You're here now. You have Meredith, and I love her. I'm glad I found you."

"If I didn't have my daughter, none of it would have been worth the pain. Honestly, I probably would have killed myself or killed him, then I would have killed myself. I was so stupid."

"Hey, don't say that. You didn't know what you were getting into. I'm sure he lied to you."

A harsh chuckle escaped her lips. "He lied so much."

"I won't lie. I can't tell you anything about my job or national security, but I won't lie. I'll tell you I'm at work, and that's where I'll be." Tony blew out a harsh breath that was full of frustration.

Audrey pulled back. "Is everything okay?"

He nodded. "It is. I'm just...I'm attracted to you, but I won't push for more until your divorce is further along. I don't want you getting in trouble for dating someone else. I don't want Meredith's future spoiled by Eddy making what we have something more than it is. I care about you, but I won't put you or Meredith at risk."

"You're too nice."

"I think you are. You're good to me, and I appreciate that."

They both rested their heads against the couch. Tony was silent for a while, and she turned her head to see if he was awake. He turned so he could stare into her eyes.

"I should go to bed," Audrey said.

Tony nodded before he leaned in, brushing a kiss over her forehead. "I'm headed that way, too. Thank you for a good day."

"I'm the one who should be thanking you. It was wonderful. I really enjoyed myself."

He gave her a hug before she turned and headed to her room. A part of her wanted to ask him to sleep with her, but she knew it was better they not develop a relationship before the divorce started processing. Once the divorce was final, she would talk with Tony and find out exactly what he wanted. She hoped he really was who he seemed to be. If he changed, becoming angry and controlling after they got together, she wouldn't be able to take it.

CHAPTER 24

Legs listened to the messages Eddy had left on Audrey's old phone. The man was unhinged. He wasn't right in his mind, and Legs was glad Audrey had flown away from the mainland and was out here on the Islands hiding from him. He'd threatened to do some rather disgusting things to Audrey. The text messages weren't any less graphic. He was glad Audrey had no access to this phone.

On Monday, Legs and his crew had extended physical training. By the time three in the afternoon rolled around, he was exhausted. He showered at the base and dressed before heading out. Mustang stopped him on the way out.

"Hey, how is Audrey holding up? I haven't seen much of you lately."

Legs chuckled. "The bullet only grazed my thigh, but I wasn't released to do physical tasks until recently. That's why I haven't been around. I've been doing clerical work and other stuff."

"Oh crap, that's awful."

"Yeah. About Audrey, she's doing good. She filed for divorce. I'm a little stressed."

Mustang narrowed his gaze. "Why?"

"I know Eddy is going to react. I just don't know how."

"Let's hope it isn't bad."

Legs had a bad feeling it was going to be terrible. He didn't want to worry Audrey, so he kept quiet when he got home. She was nervous but didn't mention anything about the divorce. After Meredith was asleep, he found Audrey in the backyard, staring up at the stars.

"He was served today."

"Are you okay?"

"I'm afraid. I know he's going to try to take Meredith. I just hope all the evidence I gave the lawyer will keep him from getting custody. I know he would do something awful to Meredith just to spite me."

There wasn't anything he could say to that. She was probably right. He would do something just to spite her. He wasn't a good person and wouldn't care if Meredith was hurt. He couldn't believe Meredith nor Audrey hadn't been offered protection. But then again, the police didn't know everything Eddy was capable of.

Close to ten, Audrey said she was going to bed. He wanted to call her back and tell her to stay with him, but he couldn't compromise her future. The judge might not be happy if Audrey started carrying on an affair with him. They might be friends and might have flirted, and they'd kissed a few times— nothing heavy—but they weren't having sex. If he went to her room and stripped off his clothes, allowing her to explore his body, that would be too much for him to hold back. He would want more.

He jerked off to thoughts of Audrey before he fell asleep. In the morning, it was raining, and he offered to drive Meredith to school, but Audrey said they could make it. He headed to work, worry filling him. Something seemed off. He didn't want to name it, but an itch in the back of his skull made him want to turn around and tell Audrey to stay at home today.

He pulled in at the base and hopped out of his truck, his mind still on Audrey and her divorce. Someone called out behind him, and he turned, spying Vine.

"Hey, you seem distracted."

Legs shook his head. "Sorry. I'll get my head on straight before I get inside. The divorce papers were served. He's going to be pissed, and I am worried."

"I'll make sure Rawlins and Tex are watching. I know you're upset, but we can't let our emotions get in the way of work."

Legs blew out a breath. "I know. I'll concentrate on work."

"Okay. We're doing a rundown of a mission a group from Virginia is running. We're there to provide support and make sure they make it out okay."

"I'm here for it."

"Good." Vine gave him a fist bump before he stepped inside.

Legs knew he needed to get his shit together. Lives were on the line. He couldn't just hope everything fell into place. He had to make sure it was in place.

The briefing was quick, but they stayed in the workroom, going over the plans the Virginia crew had made. They were rescuing a group of women and children who had been abducted in Egypt. Zero casualties was the goal, but the terrorist who had abducted them didn't care about their zero-casualty plan.

The group in Egypt was set to go in at noon Honolulu time. Worry rode him, and he went back over their plan another time. Something seemed off.

"What's up?" Vine asked.

Maverick and his team were in the room with them, all the guys watching, studying, and waiting for the team to move.

"Something is off. I don't feel right about this. Do we have a current satellite shot?"

"One is coming on in four minutes," one of the technical women from overwatch answered.

Legs moved to her, asking her to get a wide view first. The minutes ticked by slowly. His agitation grew with each passing second. Finally, the satellite was overhead, and Legs studied the image.

"What's over here?" Legs asked about one of the areas on the screen.

"That's the barn," the tech said.

Legs stood and looked at the map hanging on the wall. He had a feeling the house wasn't being used to hold the women and children. They were in the barn under the foundation. He knew military intelligence worked hard gathering data, but something felt wrong about this.

He moved back to the person on the satellite. "Look at the house and then the barn. I don't think they are in the house. I think they're in the barn."

"All of our intelligence has them in the house," one of the guys from Virginia said over coms.

"And I'm sure that's where we think they are but look at the house. The images we have don't show any bars on the windows. Why aren't people escaping?" Legs crossed his arms over his chest, then lifted his hand and chewed on his thumbnail.

The woman blew out a breath. As they watched, they saw someone walk into the field of vision and head to the barn. Why did that person go to the barn?

"Shit," the person from Virginia said.

"Great, we need to direct the SEALs to the barn," Vine said.

The person on the satellite told the SEALs what they knew. The new information was received with skepticism. Legs didn't blame them.

"The house is set with traps," Legs said. "If our guys enter, they'll be dead."

The seconds ticked by, and Legs worried he'd been wrong. His thumbnail was getting a work-over. He rolled his eyes, disgusted by his nerves, and held his hands at his sides. Then they received word that one of the SEALs had found a set of traps that the terrorists had set in the house. If they'd entered the house, it would have blown. The SEALs turned their attention to the barn. They moved slowly, entering with caution. No one was in the barn, but one of them found a door in the floor. It would be tricky getting in without taking damage. The SEALs decided to open the hatch and drop a flashbang.

With the element of surprise on their side, the SEALs headed into the hole. Legs watched, praying they all made it out okay. About ten minutes later, the SEALs called it all clear. They'd killed four terrorists, and none of the SEALs or civilians had been hit. The civilians were afraid and disoriented, but for the most part, uninjured.

Legs felt lightheaded as he stepped away from the group. Vine's hand on his shoulder stopped him.

"Man, that was great. I don't know how you knew."

He shook his head. "It just didn't feel right."

"I'm glad you figured it out. Maybe they would have seen the traps when they were close to the house, but they could have messed up. You did great," Vine said.

Everyone was happy, and he was glad he could be a part of it. Before he headed home for the day, the

SEALs were being evacuated along with the women and children they'd saved. Not every mission ended successfully, but he liked how many did.

He was almost home when Audrey called. "Do you have her?" She sounded frantic.

"Who?" Dread filled Legs.

"Meredith. She wasn't there when I went to pick her up, and they said her father came for her."

"Fuck." Legs pulled into the driveway and cut the engine.

Audrey opened the door to the house, and he ended the call. He didn't even think before he was on the phone with Rawlins.

"He has Meredith."

"What?" Rawlins asked.

Legs could hear a keyboard clicking on the other end of the phone. Then Audrey was sobbing in his arms. He squeezed her tight, praying they weren't too late to save Meredith.

"The fuck. He's still in New York. He hasn't left." More clicking came over the line. "Let me call some people. I'll get back to you."

The call ended, and Legs wrapped both arms around Audrey. "We need to call the police."

"Shit. He has her. He'll kill her."

Normally Legs and his crew would handle this,

but it was Meredith. Tears formed in his eyes as he dialed the cops. Audrey couldn't speak, so he did the talking, explaining that Audrey's daughter had been taken. This might get messy, but it couldn't be helped. They needed to find Meredith and bring her back. He just hoped the guy wasn't on a flight heading back to the mainland. They needed to stop Eddy before he destroyed Meredith.

CHAPTER 25

Audrey had no idea how long had passed. She'd run from the school back home, praying Tony was there with Meredith. When she didn't find them, she'd called Tony, hoping he had picked up Meredith and taken her for ice cream or something.

Now they were sitting around the kitchen table, talking to the FBI. It was almost midnight, and Meredith had been missing for nearly nine hours. She could be dead. That thought caused a sob that erupted and filled the small room. Tony had his arm around her again, pulling her close.

"So you didn't call the police when you found your husband killing someone."

Audrey looked at the man through tears, anger,

and pain filling her as she imagined what Eddy would do to their daughter. "He's a fucking psychopath. He would have killed us, or maybe just me. I ran when I could. Otherwise, you and your fellow agents in New York would be looking for my body. Fuck, he's going to kill her."

Tony cleared his throat. "Are you looking for Meredith?"

The agent drew in a slow breath. "Yes. She's not been on any of the planes. They're in the air long enough we checked and rechecked. There were four children around your daughter's age. We looked at photos of them boarding the planes, and then we got photos of them after they disembarked in Los Angeles or Dallas. None of them match your daughter. We've sent word to the Coast Guard. They've been tracking every boat that has left Hawaiian waters. She's still here. The police are looking. We have people out right now searching for her."

"Fuck," Audrey said again.

"This hotel in California, why didn't you tell the police what was going on?" the agent asked.

"Because he wanted to kill me. I don't know how many times I have to tell you how dangerous this man is. He will kill Meredith to get back at me. She's probably—" Audrey broke down, sobs cutting off her words.

The agent stood and left the room. Tony pulled her onto his lap, holding her close. She couldn't imagine how scared Meredith was. If she was Meredith, she would be terrified.

"Do you want anything to eat or drink?" Tony asked.

She shook her head. There wasn't any way she could stomach anything, but she knew she should be hungry. She hadn't eaten anything since lunch. There was no way she would sleep either.

The minutes turned to hours, chipping away at her hope. She wouldn't survive if Meredith died. The one bright ray of hope in her life was gone.

She used the restroom, took a shower at Tony's insistence, and finally drank some coffee as the sun started to lighten the sky. Her hands shook every time she lifted the cup. Fear and anger swirled through her.

She was outside, her thoughts bouncing from one memory to another, then pain sliced through, cutting her deep. The door opened behind her, and she turned in the chair, seeing the FBI agent stepping outside.

"Any news?"

"About Meredith, no. I'm sorry. We are still looking. It's almost noon in New York. Agents have been up there since four this morning. They've been investigating your husband for years. Based on your statement that you saw him killing someone, a warrant was obtained. The dogs hit on a few spots in the yard and under some cement poured a few years ago. They have found bones. What they didn't find was Eddy."

Tony stepped out and moved to her. "Is it Meredith?"

Audrey shook her head as she reached for Tony. He held her close, smoothing his hand over her back. If they didn't find Meredith in the next twelve hours, she knew they wouldn't find her. There were statistics about finding people who had been abducted. Statistics didn't tell the whole story, but they didn't lie. The first few hours were the most important.

The guys from Tony's team arrived along with Jenna. Audrey clung to her like Jenna was air, and all she needed was some oxygen. Words were said, questions asked, but Audrey couldn't function. Her whole life had imploded.

Close to eight, when Meredith should be going to

school, there was a flurry of activity, and a group of police officers left, racing away from the house in their cars. Audrey knew this meant something. She couldn't make herself move, though. Fear of them finding Meredith's body, broken and tossed in a ditch somewhere, filled her mind, making it difficult to even breathe.

Then the FBI agent was beside her, his hands clutching hers. "They've found Meredith, and she's alive."

"What?" Audrey asked as excited cheers went up around her. It took a moment for everyone to quiet down. Tears poured from Audrey's eyes. "How?" she asked, praying this agent was telling the truth.

"Your daughter is inventive. Apparently, she snuck out of the room the man was holding her in and ran. She said the SEALs taught her how to hike, and she remembered their lessons. She escaped and hid until she saw a police car then she ran to the officer and told her who she was. She's smart."

Audrey couldn't breathe. Meredith was safe. She turned and found Tony, pulling him into a hug. She didn't know if she was saying thank you out aloud or in her mind, but she was going to thank these men for teaching Meredith how to survive. She'd thought their survival lessons when they'd gone on hikes or when they'd played with Meredith were silly, but now she knew they'd saved her daughter's life.

They were taken to the hospital where they found Meredith happy as a clam, eating a donut and entertaining the FBI agents with stories.

"Mommy!" Meredith yelled and held out her hands.

"Oh baby, I'm so happy." Audrey wrapped her arms around her daughter, thankful she'd saved herself. Nothing mattered but her sweet child.

Meredith wanted to hug Tony, too, so Audrey let her go though it was difficult. She loved her daughter so much and had no clue how she would have survived if Meredith had been taken from her forever.

The FBI had more questions, but they let her, Tony, and Meredith go home. School and work were canceled for the day, and they sat at home, recovering from the trauma of almost losing Meredith.

Tony came outside after being inside for a moment and sat next to her. He took her hand and leaned in close, whispering, "I looked online at some articles. It looks like Eddy is in deep shit."

Her heart sped up. "Good."

"You should probably call your lawyer soon."

Audrey nodded. There was much to do, but all she wanted to do was watch Meredith play. They all napped at one point, her holding Meredith close. By seven that evening, she felt like she could breathe without breaking.

Someone knocked at the door, and Tony moved to answer. Audrey couldn't help but feel nervous as fear of someone taking away Meredith grew in her mind. She hadn't really done anything wrong, but she'd run with Meredith. Eddy hadn't reported her to the police, so they didn't count her leaving him as kidnapping Meredith, but that's technically what she'd done.

The agent they'd spoken to earlier stepped in. She didn't remember his name. At the time, the only thing she'd cared about was Meredith.

The man smiled and came over, holding out his hand. Audrey stood and shook his hand, hoping he introduced himself so she didn't have to ask his name.

"It's Agent Vinova," Tony said.

She smiled at Tony before taking a seat. "Thank you for all your help."

Vinova smiled again. "You're welcome, and thank you for all of your help. In fact, the agency wants to thank you by having you fly out to New York and interview you about everything you saw."

Panic swept through her. "What about Meredith?"

"We'll provide a hotel where you both can stay. We have a caretaker lined up. She's good and has an education degree and is a psychologist, too. Meredith will be safe while you're talking to us, and you'll have a safe place to stay. You can meet with your lawyers in New York for your divorce and get everything settled."

Audrey drew in a deep breath, unsure what she should do. Eddy needed to go away for a long time. But she hated the idea of leaving Tony. She met his gaze, and he reached for her hand.

"Go. You'll have a place here when you come back. I'm not going anywhere, and I know it'll be good to get Eddy off the streets for good."

She didn't want to leave Tony, but she had to see this through. She closed her eyes, making her decision. It would be hard to leave Tony, but she had to take care of this.

Vinova cleared his throat. "You'll have immunity. So anything you say won't result in charges."

Her eyes popped open. "I didn't do anything illegal. I had no part of Eddy's business."

"That's good. So what's your holdup?"

Audrey blew out a breath. "I don't want to leave. I haven't felt safe in years. I'm afraid going back to New York will mean Eddy can get me. I know he's in jail, but he has friends."

"We'll keep you safe. You'll be under protection."

Tony smiled, encouraging her to go. She gave a sharp nod and met Vinova's gaze. "Okay, I'll do it."

"Good. We'll set up your flight. I'll be traveling with you."

Audrey narrowed her gaze. "You will?"

"Yes. We want to make sure you're safe. We doubt Eddy will lash out right now, but we don't want to risk it. I'll call you when I have your schedule."

They all stood and Vinova turned to leave then spun back to her. "Because of your daughter's descriptions of what happened, we found the guy who took her. He'd been hired and had no clue what he was really wrapped up in. He's a career criminal. This was a violation of his parole. He'll be in jail for a long time."

"I'm glad he'll be in jail." The words felt bitter on her tongue, but that's what Eddy did. He had a way of turning everything bad. She was glad she would finally be rid of him.

Vinova left, and Audrey worried about explaining everything to Meredith. Her daughter had been through a traumatic experience, and now they were leaving Tony. She hoped this didn't damage Meredith.

"I'm going to miss you, but I'm proud of you for doing this. He needs to go away."

"He does. I just know it will be hard."

"Yes, and when you come back, you'll be that much closer to being free. And we'll be able to date."

Pleasure rippled through Audrey. "I want that."

"Good." Tony moved in close and wrapped his arms around her. He leaned back so he was staring down into her eyes. "I want to kiss you."

Butterflies erupted in her stomach as she nodded. Tony slowly leaned in so his lips were almost touching hers. He moaned softly before closing the distance. His lips brushed against hers as his eyelids closed. The kiss was slow and sensual, drawing out emotions she never thought she would experience.

When he ended the kiss and pulled back, she almost grabbed onto his neck and pulled him in for one more. This kiss with Tony would be one of her favorite memories. She would never forget the way he held her or how special he made her feel.

"When you get back, there'll be more of that," Tony said.

"I hope so." Audrey stepped back, wishing she could invite him to her bed.

Two days later, she, Meredith, and Agent Vinova left Honolulu and headed toward New York. It took a long time to get to New York, and they were all exhausted. At the hotel, she and Meredith headed up to bed while Vinova did some work.

Audrey missed Tony, but she knew she'd made the correct decision. Eddy would be put away for good, and she and Meredith would be free to live their life.

The days passed slowly at first. It took a few days to find a good time to talk. Tony kept her spirits up by sending funny memes and sweet notes. She knew without a doubt he was the man for her.

Eight days into the process of answering questions for a half-day, she felt like they were winding down. They'd been at it this morning for an hour when another agent came into the room. A sick feeling settled in Audrey's stomach. She wanted to demand they tell her everything, but she didn't have to demand anything.

The agent she'd been working with met her gaze. "I think you should know this. Someone, one of the members of a rival group, killed Eddy."

Audrey's hands flew to her face. "What?"

"He was at lunch in prison, and someone attacked him. He didn't survive."

She shook her head. "Oh, that's awful."

"I'll give you a moment," the agent said as she stepped out.

Audrey didn't know what to do. She texted Tony then called her lawyer's office. Relief poured through her. The agent came in and shrugged.

"I guess we're done. If we have any more questions, we'll contact you. An email will be sent to you about how you can arrange your travel home. Thank you for the information you gave."

That was it. She was done. She and Meredith went out for lunch, celebrating their freedom. There were no more agents watching their every move. She didn't tell Meredith why, just that they'd resolved the issue. Eventually, Meredith would learn what happened, but it wouldn't be until Audrey knew she could handle the truth. The last thing she wanted was her daughter feeling like half of her wasn't good. She may have been Eddy's biological daughter, but she wasn't anything like him.

With Eddy no longer hanging over her head, Audrey felt free. She needed to date Tony for a while, but they already had built a friendship that wasn't based on sex. Her life was good, and she looked forward to making it better as she learned to love Tony.

CHAPTER 26

Two weeks after Audrey texted Legs telling him she was free of Eddy, he stood at the airport baggage claim, waiting for Audrey and Meredith. When he spied Meredith through the glass door, he wanted to run to her, but he had to wait.

Then she was in his arms, holding his neck tight. Audrey was a little slower, but not much. He leaned over and kissed Audrey with Meredith still wrapped around him. They were a family. The start of their lives together had been wild, difficult even, but now they were together forever.

After grabbing their bags, they headed out to the parking lot. He held onto Meredith's hand as he pulled one of their suitcases. Audrey had the other suitcase and held onto Meredith's other hand.

"And we saw snow. I don't like the cold. I like Hawaii," Meredith said. "Do you think we can go to the beach soon?"

Meredith stared up at him, her eyes wide with wonder. "Yes. We can head to the beach this weekend. Everyone is excited to see you."

"Cool," Meredith said. "I hope Quirk is okay. He doesn't have anybody, and I try to help him laugh."

Legs had never heard anything that funny and burst out laughing. "Quirk will be fine. It is great that he has you, though. He needs someone smart in his life."

Meredith nodded like she had no doubt she was the smartest person in Quirk's life. He liked this girl, and he was falling for her mother. They were a part of his life now, and he was excited to find out what else their life together would bring.

He stopped beside a Jeep and Meredith narrowed her gaze. "Did you get a new car?"

"Yes and no."

Her breath hitched. "What do you mean?"

"This is the vehicle Slate told you about."

"How...wait, you didn't spend your money, did you?"

"Yes and no," he said.

She rolled her eyes. "Jesus, just give me a straight answer."

"The SEAL teams heard what happened and everyone donated a few dollars. The car is paid for and it's yours."

"You're kidding me?" Audrey gasped and stared at the Jeep, shaking her head.

"You okay?" Legs asked.

"It's perfect. This is amazing." She threw her arms around him and Meredith hugged him, too. "I can drive to work now, and drive Meredith to school."

"It's older, and we'll probably have to get some work done eventually, but it's yours."

"Thank you."

"This is great," Meredith said.

Legs picked up Meredith, kissing her cheek. "It is great. Now then, how about we head home?" He lifted his eyebrows as he looked at Audrey. "Do you want to drive?"

"Yes and no."

Legs narrowed his gaze then chuckled. "So which is it?"

"It was a long flight and I'm tired. You drive this time. I'll take it out tomorrow."

Once at home, it didn't take long for Meredith to

fall asleep. Audrey looked tired, but she said she wanted to stay up with him.

When Audrey came out of Meredith's room, they settled on the couch. She rested her head on his shoulder and sighed. Her head tilted back, and their gazes met.

"I'm happy to be home," Audrey said.

"I'm thrilled you're back."

"I guess we get to experience dating."

His lips spread wide. "I know it's odd living with me while we date. If you want, you could live with—"

"Oh no. Stop it right there. We're here. This is Meredith's home. I'm not going to drag her around anywhere else. She's already had enough trauma. We're staying."

He leaned in and brushed a kiss over her lips. "That's good to hear. I want you with me."

"So this dating thing, does that include making out on the couch?"

Legs chuckled and leaned in, sliding his tongue over her soft lips. She opened for him, sending a thrill through him. He needed to take this slow, but already his dick was hard as a rock. He stretched out on the couch beside her, loving how she fit next to him. He had been thinking of this for days.

He pulled up the hem of her shirt, and he ran his fingers over her silky skin. Pleasure rippled through him. Audrey felt perfect under his palm, and he never wanted to ruin what they had.

She moaned and arched into his touch. He wanted to give her more, but he didn't want to scare her away. She needed time to adjust.

Audrey rolled to her back and tugged him on top. The position made his body sing with pleasure. Then she rolled him to his back, straddling his legs. Her center brushed over him and he almost lost it.

After a while, both of them were breathless. Audrey pushed up and straddled him, staring down into his eyes. He reached up and cupped her cheek. Love filled him.

"I should go to bed," Audrey said.

He nodded. "You should."

"I don't want to leave you."

"I get that." Tony sat up and helped Audrey stand. He walked her over to her room and gave her a sweet kiss, wishing they were at the point he could join her in bed. It would take time, but every minute spent with Audrey would be worth it. She was his light, his hope, and he never wanted to let her go.

CHAPTER 27

Audrey had been waiting for this moment for months. She and Tony were going on a real date. Jenna and Vine were watching Meredith all night. She liked that they were open to watching her daughter though they had a child of their own. Meredith could be a handful, but both of them swore it would be no problem.

Tony arrived home, and the second he stepped into the house, her nerves took off. Would he really like her? They'd kissed and touched a little, but they would have the house for the night with no Meredith interrupting.

He had his hands behind his back, and when he came close, he moved them to the front, displaying a beautiful bouquet of flowers.

"Wow, those are amazing." She took the flowers and breathed in deeply. "These are beautiful."

"Nowhere near as beautiful as you." Tony leaned in and kissed the side of her head.

Her stomach flipped as his lips touched her hair. She was so nervous though they'd lived together for months. "Let me get these in water."

"Sure. I need to change, and then I'll be ready to go."

She heard Tony singing as he got dressed, which meant he was in a very good mood. When he stepped out of his room, he looked amazing in slacks and a dark blue short-sleeve button-down.

"I'm impressed," Audrey said.

"You look hot in your dress."

Heat filled her cheeks, and she giggled as she grabbed for her purse. Tony helped her into the SUV then hopped in on his side, his smile wide.

"You haven't told me where you are taking me."

"It's a surprise."

They pulled onto the freeway headed into Honolulu. "We're going to the city?"

Tony's lips quirked up on one side. "We are, kind of."

She watched out the windows, excitement

pinging through her as they passed the airport and headed downtown.

"I'm glad you're excited."

"Nervous, too."

"Why are you nervous?" Tony asked.

She shrugged then glanced over to him, heat racing up her neck to her face. "Because you're hot, and I'm nothing."

"Trust me, that isn't true. I think you're hot. And tonight, I'm going to have the most beautiful woman at my table."

"Where are we going to eat?"

"Oh no, I'm not telling you. It's a surprise."

Happiness filled her. "I'm fine with a surprise from you."

He reached over and took her hand, squeezing twice. He took an exit, and then they were on a winding road until he turned to the right.

"Is it close?" Audrey tried to hide her confusion. There were parking lots with chain-link fences on either side of the road, and it didn't look like any nice restaurants would be down this way.

"Trust me, it gets better in just a moment."

She reached out and touched his leg. "I do trust you."

They pulled into a lot, and she almost gasped at

how beautiful the building was. "This is amazing. Surely it's too much."

"No. I mean, we won't be eating here every weekend, but we can splurge every once in a while."

Tony came around and opened the door for her. The night grew even more magical as they stepped into the dining room, and she saw a huge mountain out the window. She turned to Tony, her mouth open. "Is that Diamond Head?"

His smile spread wide. "It sure is."

"The view is gorgeous."

They were seated with a perfect view of Waikiki and Diamond Head. The sun was just starting to set, and lights were turning on. She couldn't believe this place.

Tony was treating her too nice. She knew places like this were expensive, so she ordered what she thought wouldn't be too much. She never wanted to abuse Tony's kindness. She'd eaten at expensive restaurants and knew the person she was with was much more important than the place they took her.

"What are you thinking?" Tony asked.

She met his gaze, her heart soaring with happiness. "I think you are the person I want to spend my life with. I know I'm not supposed to say that yet. Tradition and all that stuff, but I've wasted so much time doing things the traditional way, never asserting myself or doing what I desired. Tony Caruso, I've fallen in love with you. I want to spend my life with you."

His lips spread wide, and he reached into his pocket and pulled out a simple silver band. Her heart stuttered and she grew lightheaded.

"This isn't necessarily an engagement ring, but it is a promise that we're going to get our forever after."

Audrey gasped. He really did want her. She leaned in and brushed her lips against his. They stayed with their foreheads together for a moment. When she moved to sit back, laughter spilled out between them.

"I've wanted to do this for a while," Tony said.

"Thank you." She let him slip the ring on her finger then looked at it, admiring how perfect it was in its simplicity.

"This is perfect."

He shrugged. "I can get—"

"No." Audrey shook her head and met his gaze. "I don't want something big. I want simple. I want love. I've had the other stuff, and it means nothing. Having you in my life is more important than any ring or any other possession."

He leaned his forehead against hers, letting go a ragged breath. "I love you so much."

They finished dinner with the amazing view out the window as their entertainment. Audrey couldn't believe they were at this amazing place, and she and Tony had promised forever to each other.

Driving home was one of the longest drives she'd ever taken. When he pulled into the driveway, she blew out a breath. "Thank God."

"Everything okay?"

"Yes and no." His eyebrows shot up, and she giggled. "I need to feel your naked body against mine."

He popped open his door and scrambled out. "Come on, woman. I can't keep you waiting."

Once inside, they stripped off their clothes, flinging them onto the couch. Tony stared at her for a moment, his eyes wide as he took her in. She opened her arms, and he came to her, pulling her close before ravaging her mouth.

When they came up for air, Tony said one word. "Bed."

She ran to his room, and he followed close behind, both of them laughing as they piled onto the bed. But the laughter died quickly as he kissed his way from her shoulder down to one breast then the other, circling each nipple with licks and kisses before he sucked it into his mouth.

Audrey arched up and moaned, needing his body inside hers. She spread her legs, and he began his path lower, giving her sweet kisses over her flesh, driving her dizzy with need. When he settled between her legs, he glanced up, making eye contact before he stuck his tongue out and gave her a long lick up her slit. She moaned with delight as his tongue hit her clit. She arched up to meet his mouth as he sucked and toyed with her, taking her so high she almost passed out. When she came, it was with his name on her tongue.

Tony kissed his way up her body then held above her. "I can use a condom if you like, or we don't have to."

"I'm no longer on the pill," Audrey said.

He lifted his eyebrows and shrugged. "I want babies with you."

His words filled her soul and brought a smile to her lips. "Whatever happens, happens," she said.

"I want it all with you," Tony said as he pulled back one of her knees and slid in.

Audrey gasped as he thrust, filling her completely. She thought she'd been ready for this, but her emotions almost overwhelmed her. Tony was so caring and loving, and she'd never imagined having this. She loved this man with all her heart. They didn't have what anyone could consider a traditional relationship, but what they had was more than she'd thought possible.

Tony kissed her deeply, then held her gaze as he made love to her. This was how love was supposed to feel. What they had was real, and she would never let it go.

ABOUT THE AUTHOR

Julia Bright is the author of the contemporary military romance Dark Eagle series and is an Operation Alpha Author. Julia lives in the south where "bless your heart" is an insult and "shut up" shows love. Julia has been reading since they could open a book and has taken the passion for words and combined it with the love of travel to create stories full of passion and excitement. If you love a good book with a fantastic happily ever after, you'll enjoy a Julia Bright novel. For a dash of paranormal romance and urban fantasy, pick up a book from Julia's USA Today Bestselling JS Bright pen name

facebook.com/AuthorJuliaBright
amazon.com/Julia-Bright/e
bookbub.com/authors/julia-bright

OTHER BOOKS BY JULIA BRIGHT

Finding Home

Jenna's SEAL

Ashley's SEAL

Becky's SEAL

Sunshine's SEAL

Audrey's SEAL

Fighting for Home

A SEAL for Candace

A SEAL for Deb

A SEAL for Elise

A SEAL for Trixie

A SEAL for Raven

Special Forces: Operation Alpha

Saving Lorelei

Rescuing Amy

Saving Sloan

Seeking Justice

Justice for Amber

Searching for Keeley

Justice for Oswin

Safety for Eve

Dark Eagle Series

Survive The Fall

Live Past The Edge

Hold on Through the Pain

Endure the Darkness

Storm Corp Series

Determined

Standalone Romance

Acting The Part

All Business

Just One Taste

There are many more books in this fan fiction world than listed here, for an up-to-date list go to www.AcesPress.com

You can also visit our Amazon page at:
http://www.amazon.com/author/operationalpha

Special Forces: Operation Alpha World
Christie Adams: Charity's Heart
Linzi Baxter: Unlocking Dreams
Misha Blake: Flash
Anna Blakely: Rescuing Gracelynn
Julia Bright: Saving Lorelei
Cara Carnes: Protecting Mari
Kendra Mei Chailyn: Beast
Melissa Kay Clarke: Rescuing Annabeth
Samantha A. Cole: Handling Haven
Lorelei Confer: Protecting Sara
KaLyn Cooper: Spring Unveiled
Janie Crouch: Storm
Jordan Dane: Redemption for Avery
Tarina Deaton: Found in the Lost
Riley Edwards: Protecting Olivia
Dorothy Ewels: Knight's Queen
Lila Ferrari: Protecting Joy
Nicole Flockton: Protecting Maria

Hope Ford: Rescuing Karina

Alexa Gregory: Backdraft

Michele Gwynn: Rescuing Emma

Casey Hagen: Shielding Nebraska

Desiree Holt: Protecting Maddie

Kris Jacen, Be With Me

Jesse Jacobson: Protecting Honor

Rayne Lewis: Justice for Mary

Callie Love & Ann Omasta: Hawaii Hottie

A.M. Mahler: Griffin

Ellie Masters: Sybil's Protector

Trish McCallan: Hero Under Fire

Rachel McNeely: The SEAL's Surprise Baby

KD Michaels: Saving Laura

Olivia Michaels: Protecting Harper

Annie Miller: Securing Willow

Keira Montclair: Wolf and the Wild Scots

MJ Nightingale: Protecting Beauty

Victoria Paige: Reclaiming Izabel

Debra Parmley: Protecting Pippa

Danielle Pays: Defending Sarina

Lainey Reese: Protecting New York

KeKe Renée: Protecting Bria

TL Reeve and Michele Ryan: Extracting Mateo

Deanna L. Rowley: Saving Veronica

Angela Rush: Charlotte

Rose Smith: Saving Satin
Lynne St. James: SEAL's Spitfire
Sarah Stone: Shielding Grace
Jen Talty: Burning Desire
Reina Torres, Rescuing Hi'ilani
Savvi V: Loving Lex
LJ Vickery: Circus Comes to Town
Rachel Young: Because of Marissa
R. C. Wynne: Shadows Renewed

Delta Team Three Series
Lori Ryan: Nori's Delta
Becca Jameson: Destiny's Delta
Lynne St James, Gwen's Delta
Elle James: Ivy's Delta
Riley Edwards: Hope's Delta

Police and Fire: Operation Alpha World
Freya Barker: Burning for Autumn
B.P. Beth: Scott
Jane Blythe: Salvaging Marigold
Julia Bright, Justice for Amber
Hadley Finn: Exton
Emily Gray: Shelter for Allegra
Alexa Gregory: Backdraft
Deanndra Hall: Shelter for Sharla

India Kells: Shadow Killer
CM Steele: Guarding Hope
Reina Torres: Justice for Sloane
Aubree Valentine, Justice for Danielle
Maddie Wade: Finding English
Laine Vess: Justice for Lauren

Tarpley VFD Series

Silver James, Fighting for Elena
Deanndra Hall, Fighting for Carly
Haven Rose, Fighting for Calliope
MJ Nightingale, Fighting for Jemma
TL Reeve, Fighting for Brittney
Nicole Flockton, Fighting for Nadia

As you know, this book included at least one character from Susan Stoker's books. To check out more, see below.

SEAL Team Hawaii Series

Finding Elodie
Finding Lexie
Finding Kenna
Finding Monica
Finding Carly (Oct 2022)
Finding Ashlyn (Feb 2023)
Finding Jodelle (July 2023)

Eagle Point Search & Rescue

Searching for Lilly
Searching for Elsie (Jun 2022)
Searching for Bristol (Nov 2022)
Searching for Caryn (April 2023)
Searching for Finley (TBA)
Searching for Heather (TBA)
Searching for Khloe (TBA)

The Refuge Series

Deserving Alaska (Aug 2022)
Deserving Henley (Jan 2023)

Deserving Reese (TBA)

Deserving Cora (TBA)

Deserving Lara (TBA)

Deserving Maisy (TBA)

Deserving Ryleigh (TBA)

Delta Team Two Series

Shielding Gillian

Shielding Kinley

Shielding Aspen

Shielding Jayme (novella)

Shielding Riley

Shielding Devyn

Shielding Ember

Shielding Sierra

SEAL of Protection: Legacy Series

Securing Caite (FREE!)

Securing Brenae (novella)

Securing Sidney

Securing Piper

Securing Zoey

Securing Avery

Securing Kalee

Securing Jane

Delta Force Heroes Series

Rescuing Rayne (FREE!)

Rescuing Aimee (novella)

Rescuing Emily

Rescuing Harley

Marrying Emily (novella)

Rescuing Kassie

Rescuing Bryn

Rescuing Casey

Rescuing Sadie (novella)

Rescuing Wendy

Rescuing Mary

Rescuing Macie (novella)

Rescuing Annie

Badge of Honor: Texas Heroes Series

Justice for Mackenzie (FREE!)

Justice for Mickie

Justice for Corrie

Justice for Laine (novella)

Shelter for Elizabeth

Justice for Boone

Shelter for Adeline

Shelter for Sophie

Justice for Erin

Justice for Milena

Shelter for Blythe
Justice for Hope
Shelter for Quinn
Shelter for Koren
Shelter for Penelope

SEAL of Protection Series

Protecting Caroline (FREE!)
Protecting Alabama
Protecting Fiona
Marrying Caroline (novella)
Protecting Summer
Protecting Cheyenne
Protecting Jessyka
Protecting Julie (novella)
Protecting Melody
Protecting the Future
Protecting Kiera (novella)
Protecting Alabama's Kids (novella)
Protecting Dakota

New York Times, USA Today and *Wall Street Journal* Bestselling Author Susan Stoker has a heart as big as the state of Tennessee where she lives, but this all American girl has also spent the last fourteen years living in Missouri, California, Colorado, Indiana, and Texas. She's married to a retired Army man who now gets to follow *her* around the country.

www.stokeraces.com
www.AcesPress.com
susan@stokeraces.com

Made in the USA
Monee, IL
03 March 2023